PRAISE FOR

COGNAC CONSPIRACIES

"A delightful, frequently tongue-in-cheek excursion through the mysteries and politics of cognac production.

—Live Journal

There is much to this enjoyable read."

—Librarian review

"A good story from an ongoing enjoyable series."

—Netgalley review

"So evocative of France, you can visit it in an afternoon without leaving home."

—Reader review

"The Winemaker Detective series is a new obsession."

—Marienela

"The descriptions of cognac and cigar scents and flavors drew me in as if I, too, were a connoisseur."

—Librarian review

"You deserve something different with rich flavors and aromas – You deserve this page turner."

—Reader review

"An excellent mystery series in which you eat, drink and discuss wine as much as you do murders."

—*Le Nouvel Observateur*

"A series that is both delectable for connoisseurs of wine and an initiation for those not in the know."

—*Le Figaro*

"Perfect for people who might like a little treachery with their evening glass of Bordeaux, a little history and tradition with their Merlot."

—*AustCrime*

"A wonderful translation...wonderful descriptions of the art, architecture, history and landscape of the Bordeaux region... The shoes are John Lobb, the cigars are Cuban, and the wine is 'classic.' As is this book."

—*Rantin', Ravin' and Reading*

"Combines a fairly simple mystery with the rich feel of the French winemaking industry. The descriptions of the wine and the food are mouth-watering!"

—*The Butler Did It*

"An enjoyable, quick read with the potential for developing into a really unique series."

—*Rachel Coterill Book Reviews*

Cognac Conspiracies

A Winemaker Detective Mystery

Jean-Pierre Alaux
and
Noël Balen

Translated by Sally Pane

LE FRENCH BOOK

First published in France as
Le dernier coup de Jarnac
by Jean-Pierre Alaux and Noël Balen

World copyright ©Librairie Arthème Fayard, 2004

English translation copyright ©2015 Sally Pane

First published in English in 2015
By Le French Book, Inc., New York

www.lefrenchbook.com

Translator: Sally Pane
Translation editor: Amy Richard
Proofreader: Chris Gage
Cover designer: Jeroen ten Berge

ISBN:
Trade paperback: 9781939474322
E-book: 9781939474339
Hardback: 9781939474346

"Droll Advice," *Selected Poems*, Paul Verlaine, translated by
C.F. MacIntyre, University of California Press, 1948

Drink to forget!
Cognac is one
with her apron set
to fetch you the moon

Paul Verlaine

1

With almost childlike excitement, Marie-France awaited the luminous nights when the moon carved out eerie shapes and spilled its warm light on the lush Charente landscape.

Following a cherished ritual, she would open the bedroom window wide and dreamily let her white muslin robe slip off her body and drift to the parquet floor. Then she would recline on the old sofa, which was loosely draped with Indian fabric, and for hours, sometimes the entire night, she would offer her nude body to the moonlight.

Regardless of the season, Marie-France Lavoisier was faithful to this sensuous moon-bath rite.

"It's an extraordinary way to renew yourself," she would explain to the incredulous lovers she abandoned in her bed on those nights.

She had taken up this practice years earlier, during a trip to Africa—Togo, to be precise—where a tribal chief had enchanted her with his lectures on the enormous and unknown powers of the Earth's satellite. Since then, this tenacious daughter of wine merchants from the Charente region had sworn by the sacred cycles of the moon. She was quiet and reflective during one phase, dynamic, potent, and even opportunistic the next.

Triumphantly entering her fifties, "the Lavoisier woman"—many in Cognac called her that—was still single, but so constantly pursued, she never doubted her beauty or her powers of seduction. The moon's influence, to be sure. Or at least that's what she told herself when she stood before the mirror.

She had pale blue eyes, porcelain-white teeth, delicate lips, and an alluring gaze, along with thick golden hair. When enticing a lover, she would run her long bejeweled fingers through her locks to play up this feature. Marie-France Lavoisier was convinced that she was a femme fatale and hated anyone who resisted her charms. She had one liaison after another, both one-night stands and longer affairs, with men from various social milieus. She was especially attracted to those who could benefit her cognac business, which had fallen on hard times in the vagaries of an unstable economy. Some even maintained that Marie-France Lavoisier, head of the eponymous company, had been the mistress of an important dignitary before the man became intimately familiar with the luxury of the presidential palace. At any rate, such was the gossip, undoubtedly fanned by jealous minds who resented beauty that was a touch too insolent and manipulative.

Certainly, Marie-France still had a glowing complexion, but the future of cognac in general and the family business in particular was less promising these days. The firm's problems had intensified after her father's death, when the estate was distributed, and Claude-Henri, Marie-France's older brother, had sold his shares to a group of Chinese investors. Neither Marie-France nor her younger brother—who was called "Little Pierre" even though he was in his forties—had the means to buy them back.

Claude-Henri, a good-for-nothing who was consumed by visions of grandeur, thirsty for money, and pathologically proud, had gotten it into his head to expand his wealth in Canada. Stubborn like the rest of the Lavoisier family and armed with his inheritance, he had abandoned his sister and brother one damp winter morning. Decked out like a groom, he had come downstairs as the coffee was brewing to say his parsimonious farewell. He barely uttered a word, scrutinized Marie-France in her dressing gown, and smiled before awkwardly kissing his sister and brother and promising to send news very soon.

"It's the kiss of Judas," Little Pierre had said, his eyes brimming with tears. Then he took refuge in the yard that ran all the way to the

Charente River and cried his heart out for the rest of the morning.

Marie-France, on the other hand, had gone straight to her father's office, where all decisions pertaining to Lavoisier Cognacs were made. An insipid watercolor of the patriarch overlooked a morass of paperwork piled around an opaline lamp and over an old Creys inkwell. The heiress slipped her hand under the papers and searched for the letter opener. Finding the ridiculous dagger, she fondled it for a few minutes before deciding to open the day's mail: an order from an important London restaurant that had been a faithful client of Lavoisier Cognacs for two generations, a check for a paltry amount, a customs circular, two or three advertisements, a utility bill, the latest issue of *Connaissance des arts*—that would be for Pierre—and two letters from Hong Kong. Marie-France could guess the contents and already dreaded them. She quickly and angrily slid the blade under the fold of the envelope and pulled out the correspondence.

The letter was from a Shiyi Cheng. It politely but firmly informed her that he was now a Lavoisier Cognacs board member. He was requesting a shareholders meeting within the month to provide the "Lavoisier company with the tools necessary to place it quickly among the most distinguished in the Asian market." The final paragraph stated that the Chinese investment group had hired the firm Cooker & Co. of Bordeaux to audit the business in order to "maximize the potential of Lavoisier Cognacs in a fiercely competitive environment." Cheng ended with best wishes and a pledge of his "full attention."

The second letter was from the same barrel. It was addressed to Pierre Lavoisier, Château de Floyras, Rue des Chabannes, 16200 Jarnac.

Marie-France looked at it for some time, then grabbed the vintage lighter that her revered father had used for his big Cuban cigars. It looked like a flintlock pistol. She pulled the lighter's trigger a few times before picking up the envelope and allowing the blue flame to reduce the superficially courteous wishes of the invading party to ashes.

What a mess Claude-Henri had gotten them into! Why hadn't she slapped him when he murmured, all gussied up in his three-piece suit, "At any rate, I'm a third wheel here." Then he had left through the servants' door that opened onto a mossy stairway to the yard. His footsteps had dissolved under the crunch of gravel. The gate had groaned, and a car had taken off at full speed. Had a taxi been awaiting him? Claude-Henri had left his '57 Cadillac Eldorado Brougham in the old stables. If he returned one day, she would make him pay dearly for this betrayal. How could they be related?

Marie-France collected herself after this surge of anger. She would fight tooth and nail.

In any event, she and Pierre held the majority of the shares. The vultures didn't intimidate her. A Lavoisier did not give in to epistolary demands. She had connections, after all, and knew how to use them when push came to shove.

The heiress wiped away the tears in the corners of her eyes and straightened the lapis lazuli necklace nestled against the peach-colored flesh of her throat. She ran her fingers through her hair and rushed into the rain-soaked garden.

"Pierre? Pierre? Where are you?"

Marie-France headed to the banks of the Charente. The cherry trees were in bloom, their sweet breath announcing a spring that was late in coming. But scheming gusts of wind were scattering thousands of white petals on the lawn. Her younger brother took great pride in keeping the grass more beautiful than a golf course. As Marie-France ran, the rain began to freeze. It became sleet, making the Charente waters shiver. Marie-France hadn't bothered to put on a sweater.

"Pierre? Answer me!"

There was no one on the dock. For years, this was where they had come to drown their sorrows, disappointments, and broken hearts. The pier had been used solely for that purpose ever since their grandfather and his boat had been carried off in the floods of 1966. Marie-France's father had told them that their grandpapa's decayed body was still underwater a hundred yards downstream, and a chest filled with gold coins was below deck. But the body and the boat were never found, not even during summer scorchers, when the river could be forded and children from the surrounding area would come to swim naked under the alders. Marie-France and Pierre had dreamed of recovering the treasure buried at the bottom of the river. Claude-Henri, however, never believed the story. As far as he was concerned, it was poppycock.

"Pierre? I know you're here."

Marie-France approached the boathouse. That was what they called this rotting shed used to store the fish traps, oars, reels, and rods of the last three generations. The Lavoisier family had not fished in ages, but the poles and nets were still there, tangled together and waiting for another flood to carry them off. She found her weeping brother on an old wicker bench. "Things will never be the same again," Little Pierre said. She took him by the hand the way she had on stormy nights when they were children. She nestled her head in the hollow of his shoulder. His shirt emanated the fragrance of Roger & Gallet cologne. Little Pierre was a man who wore only one scent: vetiver. She promised that she would always be by his side and that no harm could come to them, because they loved each other. She kissed him on his left cheek and sensed his pleasure. For a long while, they silently studied the needles of sleet piercing the river.

The water calmed, the wind turned east, and the storm veered toward Angeac. On the opposite bank, the acacias stopped shivering. Marie-France was snuggled beside her brother. She was united with Pierre and dreaming about the lost fortune in Grandpapa's old sunken boat.

Finally, she got up and took her disheveled brother by the hand. She led him into the wine warehouse, which smelled deliciously of eau-de-vie. This place was paradise, not unlike a holy chapel, where the family's oldest cognacs were piously stored like sacred relics. Between fits of laughter, they took in the sweet scent of prunes. It made their heads spin. Never before had the brother and sister been so united, so tenderly complicit.

In the weeks that followed, Claude-Henri was forgotten. Had he ever existed?

§ § §

A mere two hours earlier, internationally respected wine expert Benjamin Cooker had kissed his wife good-bye, swung by his offices on the Allées de Tourny in Bordeaux to pick up his assistant, Virgile Lanssien, and steered his Mercedes 280 SL toward the N10 highway. His destination was Jarnac, *haut lieu* of cognac production since the eighteen hundreds and birthplace of former French President François Mitterand.

When they arrived at the Château Floyras gate, however, no one came out to greet them. A woman's voice on the intercom informed them that they could park in the lot behind the wine warehouse. "The château is private property, and Miss Lavoisier is not seeing anyone at this time." Benjamin had not expected an overly warm reception, but to be so summarily dismissed surprised him.

Virgile was clearly annoyed. "Boss, who do they think we are: bulls in a china shop?"

"Thank goodness they didn't set the dogs on us," Benjamin grumbled as he parked his convertible in the shade of an ash tree with large drooping limbs.

"I have the feeling, sir, that the only bows we'll be getting here will be from the trees!"

"That sums it up pretty well, my boy. I am expecting the worst. That way, I won't be disappointed."

Virgile jumped out of the car, his shirt wrinkled and his hair disheveled. The trip had been rather long, and his boss's driving was far from smooth.

"Don't forget your jacket. And fix your getup. Straighten the collar and button the shirt. A little decorum, please! You'll need to use your charm to reassure the mistress of the house."

Virgile smoothed his hair and straightened his shirt. His slipped on his jacket, even though he was already feeling too warm. The early May weather tempted him to take off a layer or two, whereas Benjamin was ever faithful to his Loden, his oxford shirts, and, on this morning, his fedora, which gave him the air of an aging dandy.

"Always very fashionable, boss," his assistant said, looking him over.

"'The boor covers himself, the rich man or the fool adorns himself, and the gentleman gets dressed.' Consider yourself counseled!"

"Those are not your words, Mr. Cooker."

"That's right. Honoré de Balzac."

"Ah, yes, the guy who became disillusioned."

"You never cease to surprise me, Virgile."

They found their way to the office, which was dominated by a tall wooden staircase that smelled of polish and ambrosia. On the walls, old advertisements extolled the merits of Lavoisier Cognacs with slogans reminiscent of Radio Paris during the Vichy regime. The yellowed posters read "Lavoisier Cognac? Like velvet on the throat!" and "There is nothing more distinguished than Lavoisier Cognac!"

"Cheesy," Virgile whispered, and Benjamin put a finger to his lips. They heard footsteps coming down the stairs. An elegant-looking man appeared in a tweed vest, bottle-green corduroy slacks, and a cashmere sweater. He was holding a golden-colored flask.

"Pierre Lavoisier. Mr. Cooker, I presume?"

Benjamin shook his hand and said, "This is my associate, Virgile Lanssien."

The man, who appeared to be in his forties, adjusted his gold-rimmed glasses and gave the winemaker's assistant a thorough look-over before moving his lips almost imperceptibly. It was difficult to tell whether he was smiling or brooding.

"Beauty is the promise of happiness, is it not?"

"That's exactly what Stendhal said," replied Benjamin, always confident of his literary knowledge.

Pierre Lavoisier began to tremble ever so slightly, and sweat beads formed on his forehead. So, Benjamin thought, he didn't know how to play this game. Arrogance was not his métier, much less pedantry.

"My sister will see you, if you will kindly wait here," was all that he said before leaving. "Have a seat, please."

"We're not really tired," Benjamin responded as he inspected a large lithograph of Jarnac in 1830.

The winemaker, a connoisseur of antiques and an occasional historian, reached for his glasses. With great interest, he examined this panoramic view of a former chateau, which had been sacrificed for a suspension bridge spanning the Charente River. On the embankments, imposing homes reflected the good fortune of their owners. Along the river's edge, only a few trees dared to tip their boughs, lest they hinder the passage of the barges. Benjamin took a few steps back to better appreciate it and then turned his attention to a family photo. He recognized Pierre, standing proudly next to a beautiful woman with blonde hair. Seated in front of them was an elderly man—presumably the patriarch. Off to one side was another man, whom Benjamin presumed was the infamous Claude-Henri.

"Strange, very strange," Benjamin mumbled.

Virgile wasn't paying much attention. He was busy staring out the window at this Pierre, who had undressed him with his eyes, like a slave trader.

"There's something suspicious about him."

"What's that, my boy?"

"I'm saying that he's strange, too."

"Who?"

The door opened, and Marie-France entered the room. She was wearing a pink silk suit that complemented her astonishingly radiant complexion. Her wrists and neck were unadorned, but she had several extravagant diamond, sapphire, and ruby rings on her fingers. Her handshake was firm and formal. Ms. Lavoisier knew how to hold her own.

"So, gentlemen, what can I do for you?"

Benjamin shot a glance at his assistant before tactfully and a bit solemnly explaining the assignment he had been given. He confessed that he had not met his client, Shiyi Cheng, in person.

"We have only exchanged correspondence," the winemaker said, hoping to gain a semblance of consideration from Lavoisier. Her pale eyes were making him uneasy. "I believe your shareholder simply wishes to know the status of the accounts."

"I don't have to tell you that there are certified public accountants for that, Mr. Cooker."

She lashed out his name, and Benjamin could almost hear a whip cracking. Then her eyes fell on Virgile. She stared not at his face, but at his body, from sternum to crotch. Benjamin could feel his assistant's embarrassment. Virgile crossed his legs and pulled himself straighter in his chair as she continued her indecent and perverse inspection.

Benjamin tried to correct himself. "Perhaps I did not make myself clear, Ms. Lavoisier. Our assignment has more to do with how we can help the company evolve. We're here to study the business. Cognac is going through difficult times. I hope, in the framework of this mission, you will consider us allies, rather than enemies."

"You can be sure, sir, that I have always chosen my allies, and I don't let anyone impose them on me. Allow me to point out that your so-called mission is in no way endorsed by the Lavoisier Cognacs Board of Directors. I could throw you out, but I have too much respect for your knowledge and skills, which I know are extensive. However, Mr. Cooker, I strongly advise you not to overstep the bounds of what you call—what was it again?—your study and what we should or should not be doing to further this proposed evolution of our company."

Benjamin refused to be deterred. He employed the persuasive—and clever—diplomacy that he was known for.

"Thank you, Ms. Lavoisier, for your valuable cooperation. We will try, my associate and I, to do nothing to hinder your work, and we will foster the best possible atmosphere for a profitable collaboration. Isn't that right, Virgile?"

Marie-France Lavoisier studied the young man with the eyes of a raptor ready to dismember its carrion. Virgile, clearly aware that he was almost in the clutches of this femme fatale, managed only a stammered response: "Ma'am, our... our...interests are mutual."

"Mutual? You're getting ahead of yourself, my boy. Allow me this familiarity, because you could be my son."

"I take that as a compliment, ma'am."

"Marie-France." The woman corrected Virgile with a sweet and poisonous smile.

Virgile thrust out his chest a bit, and one of his shirt buttons came undone. Benjamin glimpsed a bit of tanned skin and pectoral muscle. Marie-France crossed and uncrossed her legs. Benjamin pretended that he hadn't seen a thing.

2

The pendulum of the old grandfather clock had a golden hue, not from the copper it was made of but from the reflection of the liquids in the large and small bottles lining the white shelves. The bottles were carefully labeled, ranked by vintages and crus: Grande Champagne, Petite Champagne, Borderies, Fins Bois.

The ticktock of the timepiece cut through the heavy silence. The sole guardian of this depository of cognacs considered it calming. A large oak table dominated the space, and spread across it was a black canvas registry. In long, broad columns, it recorded the many and varied blends. It was always in the same purple ink and careful handwriting, with capital letters dancing on the upstroke. This was Pierre's private territory, "his sacristy," as he called it with some affectation. Here, he could make reverential music with his eau-de-vie and cruets. He knew the score of every cognac and possessed an exceptional nose, which made him an authority in all of Charente and well beyond.

It was not quite noon when he heard someone enter the sanctuary without warning. Pierre was a man who practiced his religion in privacy. He couldn't tolerate being watched as he experimented with and sampled his brandy.

"Who gave you permission to enter the sacristy?" the youngest member of the Lavoisier family grumbled, turning to see Benjamin Cooker.

"No one, to tell the truth," Benjamin said. Pierre heard the apologetic tone, but that didn't matter. He didn't want him there.

"Let me work in peace."

"I promise to be quiet," the winemaker said.

"You're not being paid to be quiet. Leave immediately!"

"As you wish," Benjamin answered. "In any case, we'll run into each other before long."

"Get lost! Can I make myself any clearer?"

Benjamin put his hand on the brass knob and started to open the French door. But it got stuck. The winemaker found the pebble that was blocking his exit and kicked it away.

"Um, Mr. Lavoisier, your sister told me to ask you for the keys to the wine warehouse, but I was hoping you would accompany me. May I—"

Pierre was trembling. "You can't gain entry to our paradise just like that, even if your Cooker name is revered. You can see that I am busy."

Benjamin stomped off without closing the door. Pierre didn't care if the fine-wine expert from Bordeaux heard him swearing behind him. He took the pencil he had stuck behind his right ear like a grocer of days gone by and inscribed a formula on the dark yellow vial he had placed on the lab counter. He smiled with satisfaction as he watched the winemaker's silhouette disappear under the arbor. He was pleased that he had overcome his shyness and dismissed the man. He found him a bit too cocky.

A few minutes later, Virgile entered his sacristy. And Pierre was unable to repeat the same act of rebellion.

§ § §

Pierre's forehead was glistening, and his hands were shaking so hard, Virgile feared he would drop the vials he was holding. He looked away, as he didn't want to make the man feel even more uncomfortable.

In Armagnac a few years earlier, Virgile had learned about distillation and the art of blending, but he had never seen such a display of eau-de-vie lined up like incunabula on the shelves of a monastic library. He noticed a group of vials ranging in color from light amber to dark brown labeled with the year of his birth. He was intrigued.

"Nineteen eighty-two, right?" Pierre murmured.

Virgile smiled in agreement.

"It was a great year for Bordeaux." Pierre delivered his verdict in a tone that left no room for dispute. "Of course, there were exceptions."

"I hope I'm not one of them!" Virgile joked, walking over to the alchemist.

The man backed away, as if intimidated. A gust of wind slammed a window closed. The branches of a quince tree scraped the glass. In the distance, Virgile could see forsythia blossoms pelting the garden greenhouse.

"We're making up for what we didn't get earlier this spring. Sooner or later, you have to pay," Pierre said, reaching under the counter. He pulled out a tulip glass and ran it under the copper faucet.

"You're tall, young man. Get that vial on the upper shelf. No, not that one. The other one, the fourth from the left. There you go. Thank you very much... Gentleman—that's it!"

"I'm sorry. I'm not following," Virgile responded. "Were you calling me a gentleman?"

"No, I was referring to your cologne. It's Gentleman cologne by Givenchy, right? May I call you Virgile?"

These days, Virgile was about as faithful to his cologne as he was to his lovers. He remembered only the one he last reached for. The Givenchy cologne in his toiletry case had been a gift from Carla, the most recent woman in his life. This Pierre Lavoisier had quite a sense of smell. And to think Benjamin took him for a wet noodle. Virgile, nostrils quivering, edged toward Pierre. The older man began trembling.

"Vetiver, I'm sure of it!" Virgile pronounced. "But don't ask me the name of the perfume. I don't have your talent."

"Yes, it is vetiver. You're absolutely correct," Pierre concurred. "I use it sparingly. In my profession any ostentatious fragrance is forbidden."

Virgile noted Pierre's flattering tone and was tempted to continue complimenting this stranger, who was actually more sociable than he had thought. Still, he did not want the younger Lavoisier brother to interpret anything he said as a pass or sweet talk. So he simply sniffed the neck of the bottle Pierre was holding. The scent of prunes was intoxicating, and Pierre filled the glass of friendship one-third full. Benjamin's assistant took a sip and approved this baptism by fire with a happy face. Pierre turned the bottle around to reveal the label:

1982
GRANDE CHAMPAGNE
Blend Y 201-408-13

"Well, damn, that's good!" Virgile said.

Pierre took the glass, sipped the liquid gold, sniffed it, and savored a second sip.

"That's my glass!" Virgile joked.

"The better to share your thoughts..."

A silence ensued.

"Well?" Virgile asked, embarrassed.

"Well, I am...reassured," Pierre declared, looking at him coolly. He handed the glass back to Virgile.

Virgile did not know where to look. He studied Pierre's hand. No wedding ring. Fingernails a bit too long. Not a trace of nicotine between the index and middle fingers. This man was so featureless. An odd number. Then Virgile focused on the famous Lavoisier nose, with its excessive dark hairs, and in the space of a moment, the man became eminently likeable. Virgile emptied his glass in one swallow.

"Excellent year."

Pierre handed the bottle to Virgile. Now his hands were steady.

"Here, it's yours."

"Thank you, sir."

"Call me Pierre, will you?"

"Thank you, Pierre," Virgile mumbled. "May I ask you another favor?"

"Anything you want, if it's in my power, that is."

"A visit to the Lavoisier wine warehouse."

"Let's see if I have the keys."

Marie-France's brother made a show of feeling around the pockets of his corduroy pants. His face lit up when he pulled out an enormous bunch of keys.

"Saint Peter's keys," Virgile enthused.

"Yes indeed, these are the keys to our paradise," Pierre said as he led Virgile toward the door. He put an affectionate hand on Virgile's shoulder.

The familiarity was a stark contrast to Marie-France's coldness. But even though he had spent only a few minutes with Marie-France, Virgile could tell the two family members shared some characteristics. They were both aware of their seductive power and the effects their charm had on others. Each made ample use of it and knew it worked equally well on both sexes.

§ § §

Benjamin was in a heated discussion with Marie-France when he spotted Virgile and Pierre passing beneath the arbor on the way to the moss-covered wine warehouse. He wanted to see the company's books and the rest of the records, but Marie-France was refusing to budge. He would have to wait.

It was lunchtime, and the winemaker needed food to soothe his exasperation. Virgile was off with Pierre, so he sought refuge by himself in a restaurant on the Rue du Chêne-Vert. He ordered a steak that he shamelessly enjoyed with a glass of 2001 Maine des Aireaux. Benjamin would definitely include this Domaine Brillet in the next edition of his guide. And to think the Charente region was so often dismissed as a brandy-only producer.

§ § §

Pierre Lavoisier turned the key. A cool, moldy smell greeted them. Pierre switched on the light, sending shadows across the gray walls of the immense nave. It was lined with stacks of casks marked in chalk. Virgile silently walked behind Pierre as he pointed out the various barrels. The entire Lavoisier treasure, accumulated over the course of more than two centuries, was before them, standing at attention and ready to be shipped off to the Americas and the Far East, provided, of course, there were buyers. Along with James Delamain and Thomas Hine, the Lavoisiers were the founders of the eau-de-vie business in Jarnac. Under Napoleon, they had known some reversals of fortune. But through all crises, they had managed to survive and ward off ruthless bankers. After the two world wars, they had wisely and stubbornly refused to merge with sweet-talking unscrupulous brands.

Pierre explained all this while strolling along the rows of barrels. He mentioned the wine cellar fungi—often called "angels"—the ethylic vampires that sipped at least five percent of the reserves. Pierre raised his eyes toward heaven, as if imploring God to keep the mischievous seraphs from taking too much. But what Virgile saw when he looked up was just more mold.

"I know all these black spots have a useless Latin name," Virgile said, grinning at the opportunity to show off some of his own knowledge. "Torula something or other."

"*Torula conglutinate compniacensis,*" Pierre replied. He headed toward a rusty gate, behind which demijohns were nestled in straw. "And tell me, Virgile, what is the propagating agent for this strange fungus?"

"Oh please, Pierre, you remind me of Mr. Cooker with your two-buck questions. It's a spider that proliferates in alcohol vapors. A wino, you could say. Call it what you like."

"If we called it *Arachnea compniacencis*, we wouldn't be far off. You can ask your Mr. Cooker tonight."

Virgile tried to move away from the man, who kept touching his arm, as though knowledge were passed via his fingers. The reluctant apprentice approached the locked gate, expecting to enter what he sensed was the holy of holies.

Pierre turned to Virgile, looking him in the eye. "Nobody forces their way into paradise. Here you need a guide."

He flipped a switch that turned on a string of old lightbulbs. "Everything is indexed, itemized, numbered, and codified. We have nothing to hide."

With the space illuminated, Virgile could see that the demijohns in this damp cellar were draped with spider webs, which spanned decades and even centuries. Some of these vessels had rubbed shoulders with Chateaubriand, Balzac, Napoleon III, Hugo, and the Romanovs. Virgile was speechless. He had the sense that he was standing before the Shroud of Turin. On the back of his neck, Virgile could feel the excited breath of his mute companion. He was so close, Virgile didn't dare turn around.

"Virgile?"

"Yes," Virgile answered. A minute earlier he had been standing on the threshold of paradise. Now he was smelling sulfur.

"I wanted to tell you that—"

"That what?"

There was a long silence.

"That even if you are being paid by the Asians, I won't hold it against you."

"I thank you for your trust, Mr. Lavoisier."

"Won't you call me Pierre?"

"Thank you...Pierre."

Virgile looked for the shaft of light that had led them to this cellar full of bulging casks and voracious spiders. He made for the exit with the swift foot of a thief. Pierre Lavoisier was hot on his heels, like a priest pursuing a poor sinner resistant to absolution.

Outside, the sun was drenching the soft grass. The wind had stripped the cherry trees of their petals, but the golden chain trees were giving out their first yellow clusters in an orgy of heady fragrances. Virgile announced that he was ravenous. Pierre offered to share a soup of garden snails and wild nettles. Virgile was hesitant to accept, but he couldn't say no to escargots. Benjamin had a weakness for frog legs, but Virgile would sell his body for a plate of snails. Oscar Wilde, allegedly his employer's great-great-uncle, was right: better to submit than resist!

3

After his meal, Benjamin asked the pimply waiter to bring him a Lavoisier cognac. The unattractive youth in a barely clean shirt apologized profusely. It was a rare brandy that was hardly ever offered at this establishment, whose patrons were mostly business people in a rush. The winemaker was disappointed but accepted a Frapin VIP XO while he took a Cohiba Siglo VI from his shark-skin case. Thick billows of smoke isolated him from the rest of the room, where a few customers were hastily gulping down a second cup of coffee. This quarantine pleased him; each puff fanned his reflections.

This business was beginning to seem like a bad undertaking. Shiyi Cheng had already asked for a report in an e-mail that had arrived that very morning at Benjamin's Allées de Tourny office. Benjamin had asked his devoted secretary, Jacqueline, to respond with a quote from the French Renaissance writer François Rabelais: "Everything comes in time to those who can wait."

Being in Jarnac, his initial thought had been to quote François Mitterand, who was known for saying, "Give time the time it needs," but he had decided against it.

The winemaker had naively assumed that his client would be patient and wise. Weren't these Eastern virtues? But the Chinese investors were keen on his fully detailed conclusions. The underlying objective was becoming clear: to determine if they should pick up even more shares of this presumably undervalued company. Without the complete cooperation of the Lavoisiers, Benjamin would be forced to delay his preliminary report. Unless Virgile, armed with the audacity of youth and an angelic face, proved to be a better sleuth.

Despite his concerns, he sent up thanks for the marriage of cognac and Cohiba that he was now enjoying. The restaurant owner, having recognized him, cheerfully offered another glass. Benjamin declined, paid the bill, and took his smoky meditations to the banks of the Charente. He strolled down the Rue du Château to the Quai de l'Orangerie. He walked past the Bisquit cellars and the House of Hine as he looked for a bit of shade. But there weren't many trees along this wharf, where salt was once unloaded, and cereals, wines, and fine eau-de-vie were shipped out.

The fruity notes of Benjamin's cigar had given way to the subtle scent of cacao. The winemaker had slowed his pace and was contemplating the Tiffon cellars on the left bank. The building looked like a beached ocean liner with its rows of arched windows mirrored in the unruffled waters of the river. Benjamin remembered an old Jarnac merchant's history lesson about this stone structure. It had been built in the eighteen seventies for the House of Vert & Cie, which had been forced to surrender all its cellars to the Tiffon firm, founded in 1875 by a certain Médéric Tiffon.

The meditation brought him full circle to the Lavoisier family. What strange dynamics he'd felt there. Why had Claude-Henri sold his shares? To get away from his shrew of a sister and his weakling of a brother?

Benjamin savored his cigar to the last third before throwing it into the water. He watched the core float to the surface, but then a dinghy distracted him. A woman of indeterminate age was at the steering wheel, proudly smoking a cigarillo. She had red hair and was tall and slender. Benjamin thought she looked like the actress Claudia Cardinale. As she drew closer to the lock, Benjamin could make out a companion and hear the woman letting out little squeals of pleasure. The companion was holding her hips and pecking her on the neck. Their happiness was so out in the open, but their small boat seemed too fragile.

Benjamin's heart wasn't in his work. He decided to take a drive. After all, Virgile seemed motivated enough. He retrieved his convertible, and once he had crossed the bridge, he took the D141 road toward the town of Cognac. The winemaker stopped briefly to put the top down. The air was full of the sweet fragrance of mock orange, and there wasn't a cloud in the sky. He slipped his Carmen CD into the player and listened to "The March of the Toreadors." Bizet was a perfect companion when one needed an escape from serious thinking.

Benjamin finally forgot his disagreement with Marie-France. That night, in the impressive eau-de-vie library at the Château Yeuse hotel and restaurant, he would order his Lavoisier cognac. Perhaps he would sip it while listening to Virgile's account of his investigation thus far. He sincerely hoped—for Virgile's sake, as well as his own— that his assistant was keeping his well-trained nose clean.

In the town of Cognac, the winemaker parked with some difficulty near Place François I. He went to the Maison de la Presse to buy newspapers and magazines and, still in his Loden, took a seat on the terrace of the Coq d'Or. He ordered a lemon Perrier before taking the top off a cigar. He perused *Vinomania* with a cynical eye, as if he already knew the contents and final verdicts of the tasters, some of whom—not that he cared—were his most ardent detractors. In the end, he was supremely bored with all the wine industry news. Only the *Revue des Vins de France* and *La Vigne* met with his approval. He set aside his reading and amused himself by studying the buildings and watching the small town's residents parade by.

Cognac had known prosperous times. Fortunes had been amassed on the banks of the hard-to-tame Charente River. Dynasties had been built in the wake of barrels carried off on its waters. Wars, dissension, and unfortunate associations had destroyed some of these dynasties. One could still make out the names on the walls of abandoned wine cellars. Other well-known families, hoping to salvage what was left of their honor, had found themselves under the heel of large companies, and the old cellar masters had been forced to turn in their aprons.

The town of Cognac maintained a certain Napoleonic pride, with its slate roofs, pretentious gables, ceramics memorializing illustrious founders, stucco cornices, winter gardens, and generally polished ambience. But alongside the gated residences were atrocious buildings, where cement rivaled glass in a burst of modernity meant to be a sign of progress. Benjamin thought it was a glaring example of poor urban planning.

Most of Cognac's luster was now faded. A few wine merchant companies boasted authenticity but produced only advertisements. The myriad billboards at the edge of town, touting cognac and pineau as elixirs, seemed vulgar.

But the true and unique aristocracy of Cognac still survived in Jarnac. The Lavoisier family belonged to that lineage: daring and resolute, discreet and fiercely unyielding. Marie-France's character had been forged from these values, which stood in danger of extinction. Benjamin told himself that he should never have agreed to work with the foreign investors. It was a matter of ethics. Perhaps it wasn't too late to back away.

A woman sat down at the next table. She was wearing a straw hat, faded jeans, a pair of necklaces, and designer sunglasses. It was obvious by her affected gestures and the freckles visible above the low-cut neckline of her sweater that she was a foreigner. Irish perhaps or, more likely, English. Benjamin could detect his compatriots as easily as his setter could find a rabbit in a field of tall grass. He lowered his reading glasses and studied his neighbor. The foreigner took off her tinted glasses and revealed heavily made-up eyes, which were almost turquoise.

"Oh my God! Can it be? Benjamin! You're Benjamin Cooker, aren't you?"

Even more than the blue-green eyes, the voice resonated in the winemaker's memory, like an old melody or a musky perfume. It was the strange music of an Oxford accent. For a few seconds, Benjamin remained speechless. Then he uttered the name he had never truly forgotten: "Sheila! Sheila Scott."

The English woman burst out in laughter, rushed over to Benjamin, and threw her arms around his neck with such effusive affection, he was almost embarrassed. She nearly smothered him before pulling herself away and patting his chest and shoulders, as if trying to convince herself that this reunion was not a dream.

"Ben! My Benjamin. You haven't changed one bit. Just a little heavier and a few gray hairs! My God, I don't believe it. You, here, after all these years. You know, I often see your picture in the paper, but I never dared to get in touch with you. All that is ancient history. We were just kids. How old were we again?"

Benjamin was a little taken aback and pretended to ponder the question, even though he was well aware of the answer.

"Nineteen. It was our first year at art school. You had beautiful blonde hair, and your French was not great, but you sure could draw. Even the drawing professor was a bit in love with you."

"I remember that tiny, top-floor closet your father rented for you in that chic neighborhood: the Avenue Raphaël in the sixteenth arrondissement. You were already living like a king with all that cash you were getting from London. The bohemian life wasn't for you. And there I was, modeling for magazines. I had to bare my chest to make ends meet!"

"You used to tell me you enjoyed that," Benjamin replied, his eyes full of mischief as he tried to relight his cigar, which had gone out during the burst of memories.

"Just as naughty as ever, my Ben! I'll bet your wife doesn't get bored with you."

"You'd have to ask Elisabeth yourself. In any case, if she were, I'm sure she wouldn't let on," Benjamin quipped, confident of the charm he still exercised over this love of days gone by. The two English compatriots had met in Paris under the glass roofs of the École des Beaux-Arts. Both of them yearned to express themselves in more than their artwork. Their common language, their youthful and vigorous bodies, their shared passion for the Impressionists, and a sweltering September had transformed the room on the Avenue Raphaël into a licentious suite for lovers. The once-proper Brits remembered their upbringing well enough to cry out "God!" at every opportunity in their couplings and even managed to arouse their landlady, a hardened spinster doomed to solitary pleasures.

"Blasting Kiss and Aerosmith on your cassette player wasn't enough to drown out our noise!" Sheila said, motioning to the waiter. "Two glasses of Champagne, please." Benjamin noticed that her milky skin was already turning pink in the sun.

"Fortunately, my love affair with heavy metal didn't last." He turned to the waiter and asked in the tone of a customer who could not be fooled, "What do you suggest?"

"Uh, we have Mumm, Moët, and Gosset."

"Gosset will be perfect," Benjamin said. He had thrown off the poor young man, bestowed by nature with a cleft lip.

"Honestly, you haven't changed a bit. You leave nothing to chance."

"That's not true. Otherwise, we would never have met again!" Benjamin joked. He took a puff of his Dominican cigar. "May I ask what you're doing in Cognac?"

"I've been living here for almost ten years now. That is, not exactly in Cognac—in Migron. It's a little village twelve miles from here. I restored an old water mill. I love it there."

"Excuse me if I'm prying, but do you live alone?"

"After Styron died, I decided not to have another man in my life."

"You were married?"

"As good as. I can assure you, he left me everything. Even now I'm living on his royalties. It's enough to get by. I would so love for you to come to Samson's Mill. That's the name of my place."

"So that you can be my Delilah for a night?" Benjamin immediately regretted his words. Charming was one thing—suggestive was quite another. He squirmed in his seat.

"Some embers are better left unstirred." Sheila sighed as she slid a hand into the neck of her cashmere sweater to adjust a bra strap.

The waiter placed the two glasses of Champagne on the table. A brown birthmark ran down his neck, and he hunched his shoulders as if to conceal this other congenital affront. Although Benjamin detested pity, he would shell out a generous tip.

"Is it cold enough?" ventured the young man.

"It's perfect," Sheila said with a lovely smile.

The two friends raised a toast, exhumed buried memories, and roared with laughter at the childish antics of their late teens and early twenties.

It had turned out to be a beautiful afternoon, after all. Benjamin promised to visit Sheila at teatime the following day. The recollection of these tender years had made him happy and even aroused guilty feelings regarding his assistant.

But at Château Yeuse that evening, he said nothing about his encounter. He was quiet at dinner and just played with his *pigeon de Gâtine*. Even its perfectly rosy flesh could not whet his appetite. He told Virgile that he had taken a short stroll along the banks of the Charente River and spent some time on his guide. His editor had been uncharacteristically critical of the latest chapter.

"You don't seem yourself, boss," Virgile finally said, after telling him everything about his conversation with Pierre Lavoisier. "Is it that argument with the Lavoisier woman that's bothering you?"

"Not exactly," Benjamin replied listlessly as he sipped a Léoville Poyferré that should have remained in the wine cellar a few more years.

"Nothing serious, I hope."

"It's really nothing. Maybe it's just this Saint-Julien wine, which is way too young. Or maybe it's fatigue, the annoyances, and my impatience to get back to Grangebelle."

"We've just gotten here, and you already want to wrap up the assignment and leave? You're in a hurry, Mr. Cooker, and that's not like you."

"Just a bit weary, Virgile. Don't mind me," he said. He folded his napkin, indicating that dinner was over, and he had no desire for dessert, coffee, or even a cigar.

He left the restaurant without a word. Virgile followed him out to the terrace, which overlooked the château's lush hanging gardens. The scents of wild mint and chamomile floated in the night air.

"Isn't it nice here?" Virgile said. Benjamin could tell he was trying his best to sound enthusiastic.

The two men watched the lights of Cognac beyond the river. The moon was spilling its silver luminescence on the sleepy water. The air was a bit cool but not at all humid.

"It's beautiful, isn't it?" Virgile said again.

Benjamin turned up the collar of his Loden and leaned against the railing. "Charente: it's the most beautiful stream in my kingdom," he said dramatically.

"Who said that?" Virgile asked. There was an almost teasing tone in the question.

"King Francis I," Benjamin replied smugly.

"Wrong!" Virgile responded, clearly proud of catching his mentor in a mistake. "Henry IV! Pierre quoted that line this afternoon. He's a bit of a historian, too."

"He's a bit of a lot of things, that Pierre Lavoisier. And you accept everything he tells you at face value? Where's your discernment, Virgile?"

"Sir, you have a lot of preconceptions about the Lavoisiers. I think we are not going to agree on anything tonight. We should just call it a night."

Benjamin's feathers were ruffled, and this only exacerbated his gloomy mood. "You're absolutely right, Virgile," he said. Benjamin pulled away from the railing and disappeared into the darkness, leaving the crunch of gravel as his only good night.

4

Toward Royan, a storm was racing across the hills at the speed of a galloping horse. Clouds bursting with moisture were heaped on the horizon. Benjamin thought they might even be full of hail as he sped along the road. Luxuriant flowering vines greeted him at every bend, and his 280 SL skidded when he negotiated a turn too abruptly or was distracted by a bell tower. He stopped in Villars-les-Bois to admire the tympanum and eight-centuries-old leopards of the beautiful Romanesque church. He said a prayer and took a walk through the grassy cemetery. After checking the oil in his convertible, Benjamin started toward Migron at a more deliberate speed. He wasn't in a hurry to get to his destination.

Benjamin realized that he should have declined the invitation, but he had allowed his reunion with Sheila to take his mind off his work. He knew now that he had to drop the assignment, and in a matter of hours, he would be done with it.

On his way out of Cognac, Benjamin had bought some pastries and asked the salesgirl to package them nicely. For a fleeting moment, he had considered taking roses, but thought better of it and had stolen away from the florist's shop like a villain.

Benjamin stopped for directions just a few miles from Samson's Mill.

"It's not far away, my good fellow," an old man with rheumy eyes and drunken breath told him. "It's on the right, just as you leave town, after the sign for Burie."

An old wooden gate covered with exuberant trumpet vines marked the entrance to Sheila's place. Benjamin took the long dirt road sheltered by hazelnut trees. He crossed one bridge and then another before coming to a halt in front of a fortress of impenetrable rosebushes bustling with bees. He could barely make out the roof and blue shutters of the structure perched atop a trickle of water that could hardly be called a stream.

Samson's Mill gave off the aroma of old England. It reminded Benjamin of Drayton Gardens in the south of London, where, as a child, he would visit one of his father's old aunts. She was as ugly as a scarecrow, but her mansion and garden were blanketed with honeysuckle, wisteria, and white iceberg roses that were tinged with pink in the last hot days of summer. Their charm made him forget about the aunt's looks, and the fragrances overpowered her smell of cat pee.

Everywhere Benjamin looked, there was a profusion of plants. The gazebos, porticos, and pergolas were laden with them.

Sheila, in a straw hat and oversized boots, emerged from behind a vine-covered trellis. She was also wearing a T-shirt that read, "Without music life would be a mistake." The woman apparently didn't bother to wear a bra while she was gardening, because Benjamin could make out the two rosebuds of her proud breasts. Time had not diminished them in the least.

"Oh, Ben! Here you are, finally."

Sheila dropped her pruning shears and rushed over to greet her old friend. She planted her lips on both of Benjamin's cheeks. He felt a bit ridiculous with his *baba au rhum* in hand. And her warm welcome wasn't exactly soothing his qualms about being there.

"The weather is unbearably oppressive," she said. "Go ahead, take off your coat. Let me show you my kingdom. Oh, I can feel some raindrops already. The storm will relieve some of this humidity, but I hope it doesn't destroy my rosebushes."

Sheila took Benjamin by the arm and led him along the paths of her rose garden. She pointed out each of her treasures, some of which were just starting to bloom. Here was an Arethusa, a rose from China with apricot-colored double flowers. Over there was an Archduke Joseph, a tea rose, and farther on was a Baron de Gossard, a hybrid with beautiful purple flowers verging on violet.

"My garden's magnificent until the last days of autumn," she said.

Benjamin was impressed with her knowledge. She was even able to give the Latin name of each specimen.

"And this one here?" Benjamin pointed to a tall shrub whose leaves were trembling in the west wind.

"That bush? That's the Belle de Crécy. A Gallic rosebush that produces extremely fragrant flowers."

Samson's mistress did not let go of Benjamin's arm as she pulled him deeper and deeper into her garden. They came to a Japanese bridge. They leaned over the railing like two reckless kids and spotted a school of fish in the clear water. Benjamin's head spun with all the information on pruning roses, protecting them from predatory insects, and supporting them with stakes.

"Here is the pearl of my garden," Sheila said, pulling him closer. "It's a rarity in the West. It's the *Rosa yakushimanense*, a rambling Chinese rosebush."

"I just can't get away from them," Benjamin muttered.

"What did you say?"

"Nothing, really. I'm doing some work for a Chinese client."

At the moment, the winemaker didn't want to talk about his work. "Tell me, does your *rosa-yaku-*whatever tend to prick when you get too close?"

"Yes, it has lots of sneaky thorns," Sheila said.

"Oh, I know the type!"

It was beginning to rain harder. Benjamin and Sheila took shelter under a cherry tree. The rain soon became a downpour, pummeling the garden tables and plants.

"As hard as it's coming down, we won't get the brunt of the storm," Sheila said. "It's heading for Angoulême." The Cognac transplant sounded quite sure of her prediction.

"I put myself in the hands of Samson's prophetess!" Benjamin said. Still, he looked for lightning before edging farther under the limbs of the tree. The last thing he needed was to get struck by a thunderbolt in his old flame's garden. Sheila wiped the wet hair off her face. The shape of her breasts was even more pronounced under the wet cotton T-shirt.

"We should make a dash for the house," Benjamin suggested after a brief silence.

"No, let's stay here. Don't you find it exciting, lightning and all?"

Sheila let out a deep laugh, which Benjamin didn't quite understand. He was at a loss to respond. Years earlier, beneath the glass roof of the

Beaux-Arts school on the Quai Malaquais, she had made the first move, stunning him with a languorous kiss so unlike the pecks he had experienced to that point in his young life. He had closed his eyes and surrendered.

Lightning struck not very far away, near Villars-les-Bois. Benjamin wondered if it had hit the bell tower of the Romanesque church. The thunder that followed sent the rose gardener into Benjamin's arms. He could feel Sheila Scott's hot breath through his pinstriped shirt.

"Sheila, do you have any Grand Yunnan? I could use some tea."

The Englishwoman pulled away from the chest where she had sought refuge. She picked up her straw hat, which had fallen to the ground, nimbly pushed her hair back in place, straightened her T-shirt, and ignored Benjamin as they made their way past the sodden rose bushes.

Once inside the house, Sheila slid a battered kettle onto the burner of the old gas stove. She was no longer the effervescent hostess. Her movements looked weary.

"Poor Ben, I only have green tea."

Standing in the doorway, Benjamin watched the storm trail off over the hills of Rouillac. "That will be fine," he said.

§ § §

"Mr. Cooker, sorry to bother you, but I haven't heard from you, and you've left me with no instructions. You promised to stop by the Lavoisiers's this afternoon. Things aren't so comfortable here. I persuaded the brother to put his cards on the table. His sister doesn't know it, but he showed me the books, and you know balance sheets are not my thing. I'm at a loss. Please get back to me."

Benjamin smiled when he listened to the three rambling messages a nervous Virgile had left on his phone, which all said more or less the same thing. Apparently, the more information, secrets, and clues Virgile obtained, the more panicky he felt. But tomorrow, all this would be irrelevant. Benjamin would be calling Shiyi Cheng in the evening to announce his resignation. He would reimburse him to the last dime for the initial fee he had collected. Benjamin would say he was leaving for personal reasons and would give no more explanation than that. His mind was made up.

Virgile would undoubtedly be disappointed. Just when the secret world of eau-de-vie was opening up to him, Benjamin was hijacking the friendship he had established with the most famous nose in Cognac. This injustice would infuriate him. Benjamin was prepared for a frosty reception at dinner.

When the winemaker attempted to reach his assistant, the "no service" message appeared on the screen of his cell phone. Could the storm have disrupted this too?

Benjamin hurriedly left Samson's Mill, loudly revving the six cylinders of his convertible and ignoring the puddles along the hazelnut-tree-lined drive. Just as he neared the end of a drive a shiny Renault turned in. Curious, he slowed down and watched. The car stopped at the house, and a sloppily dressed man who looked to be in his thirties climbed out. With designer luggage in tow, he started walking toward the front door.

Benjamin shrugged. Sheila's business was not his. He sped up again, heading toward Cognac. On the ring road that bypassed the city, the 280 SL veered right. Jarnac was only a cannon shot away. The sun reemerged and spread its honeyed rays over the rain-drenched vines in a way that made nature seem unreal. Benjamin thought of Sheila's rosebuds and played recklessly with the accelerator until he saw flashing blue lights in the rearview mirror. He pulled over, braked, and returned to reality. Elisabeth would never forgive him.

§ § §

"Who's that old dude in the sports car?" the man asked Sheila, who was smoothing her hair.

"Back so soon, Nathan? Oh, he's one of your father's best friends. I don't think you ever met him. He is vacationing in Royan, and he surprised me with a visit. I hadn't seen him in such a long time. I hardly recognized him."

"I don't like his looks."

"He's quite respectable."

"I said I don't like his looks. He had no right inviting himself here."

"It was just a friendly visit."

"I hope so."

Only then did Nathan kiss his mother.

"What's the matter? You're crying."

"It's amazing how much you resemble your father."

§ § §

The evening did not unfold as Benjamin had imagined. Points on his license, a stiff fine, and an awkward rendezvous with a former lover—all this had disturbed the winemaker so much, he had forgotten to call his client. Virgile's boundless admiration for the youngest member of the Lavoisier family couldn't draw Benjamin out of his foul mood. Even the 1989 Saint-Julien Chasse-Spleen, not only impeccable but also served at the perfect temperature by Maria, the Yeuse sommelière, had no effect. Decidedly, Charente was not where he wanted to be. Tomorrow, he would put an end to this audit, at the risk of incurring the wrath of the East. But he would win back the esteem of Marie-France, and, above all, he would be able to get back to Grangebelle and his wife's affections.

After the meal, Benjamin retreated to the eau-de-vie library. He hoped a Magnum 46 cigar with an oily cap would bring him out of his ineffable funk. At one thirty in the morning, he said good night to the watchman and stumbled back to his room. Hiccupping, the renowned wine expert and author looked in the bathroom mirror. Staring back was a glassy-eyed man with disheveled hair and smudges on his shirt.

§ § §

A fog hung over the Charente landscape without settling on the sentry-like poplars. The scent of freshly cut fennel was rising from the earth as Benjamin and Virgile headed toward Château Floyras. Virgile rolled his window down. Benjamin followed suit and inhaled the vegetation. The fresh air was sobering him up, and he would have taken the top down, but he knew it would bother his assistant.

Coming into Jarnac, the Mercedes rushed down the Rue Maurice Laporte Bisquit to the Rue Chabannes. Benjamin quickly braked when he spotted two fire trucks and an ambulance blocking the narrow road. At the corner of the Rue des Moulins, men in wet suits were making their way back to their truck with disappointment written on their faces. The battle was over. Firefighters in blue uniforms trailed behind. Four paramedics were tending to the limp body of a man lying in his own vomit on a gurney.

Benjamin was tempted to get out of the convertible to see what had happened. It was clear that the man was dead. Virgile grabbed his sleeve to stop him.

"Don't move, sir. I have a bad feeling."

Benjamin obeyed but was taken aback when Virgile climbed out of the car himself and walked over to a police officer standing next to the paramedics and the gurney.

Virgile seemed to lose his balance and sought a wall for support. Benjamin got out of the car and rushed to his assistant.

"Do you know him?" he heard the officer ask Virgile.

"Yes, it's Pierre Lavoisier. I recognized the Cartier Tank watch on his wrist."

"Come away now," Benjamin said, putting his arm around Virgile to hold him up. "You shouldn't be looking at this."

The storms of the previous day had swollen the Charente River, and the water mills were making a thunderous noise—a stark contrast to the stunned silence in the car.

5

Benjamin and Virgile had retreated to the Château Yeuse as the small world of Cognac took in the news. Virgile had made it clear that he intended to stay for the funeral, and Benjamin didn't feel right about leaving him on his own. Besides, he knew he should attend the service too. In record time—a demonstration of the Lavoisier family's standing in the town, Benjamin thought—Pierre Lavoisier's death was ruled an accident, and the service was scheduled.

Benjamin and Virgile took seats at the back of the church. The winemaker, who, unlike his assistant, was in the habit of attending church, found the service as boring as the clear-glass windows. The light was much too harsh. He surveyed the mourners. Two envoys sent by Shiyi Cheng all the way from Hong Kong were trying to follow the liturgy, without much luck. The bigwigs of Cognac were in the front pews. Although he couldn't get a good view, he could imagine their gloating faces and read their minds: Didn't the arrogant Lavoisier family deserve to be neglected by God, just a little?

The mourners sitting with Virgile and Benjamin at the back of the church weren't dressed as well as those in the front pews. These people were the ordinary inhabitants of the winemaking world. For decades, many of them, residents of Grande and Petite Champagne, had delivered their grapes to the Lavoisiers. They were certainly wondering if their contracts would be honored, as the future of the business appeared to be in jeopardy.

Benjamin was surprised to see Sheila Scott in the church. She smiled, and once again, he took note of her alluring turquoise-blue eyes. Black, however, did not become this English beauty with porcelain skin. Next to her was a rather elegant-looking man with graying temples and a Legion of Honor pin on his lapel. He had to be some sort of government official or the head of an agricultural cooperative. He looked vaguely familiar. Perhaps he was a former minister, but Benjamin didn't hold politicians in particularly high esteem. At regular intervals the smug-looking man gave the rose grower a lustful look. Benjamin swore he saw her batting her eyelashes at the man, whoever he was. The younger man Benjamin had seen driving up to Sheila's house earlier in the week wasn't in any of the pews.

At the end of the service, six employees of Lavoisier Cognacs picked up the heavy coffin and carried it down the long nave and into the tepid May sunlight.

Walking a few steps behind the oak coffin, Marie-France looked stunning in her sober black suit. Outside, the light breeze that tossed her blonde hair sent ripples over the waters of the nearby Charente.

§ § §

The beams of bright light cast by the blood-red moon did not reach the bed, and Marie-France couldn't muster the strength to drag herself to the sofa to offer her body to the orb's embrace. She was exhausted, and her bones ached. The day had been grueling. All those aggrieved faces. The procession of deceitful acquaintances saying the same thing: "I'm so sorry" and "We all loved him so much." The limp, sweaty palms and the hugging, so common in mourning, with the inevitable whiffs of eau de cologne. The whole hypocritical ritual had left her undone.

Pierre Lavoisier's funeral Mass had filled the Saint-Pierre church with a crowd that spilled into the square. The entire cognac world had come together to view the event. Who would have missed it? After all, this was more than the funeral for a key member of one of the region's most illustrious families. What the people here were witnessing was quite possibly the death of Lavoisier Cognacs. The Chinese would certainly jump in and pay top dollar for the shares the renegade brother would inherit—the one who had fled to God knows where with God knows whom. Claude-Henri hadn't even bothered to show up for his brother's funeral. His absence, noted in hushed voices, spoke volumes. And how! The siblings had to hate one another not to reconcile when death swooped down and snatched one of their own. The Lavoisiers had failed to keep up appearances in this tradition-steeped land. Who could imagine a worse downfall?

Left with no one to rely on, Marie-France had made the arrangements by herself. She had orchestrated the funeral, chosen the hymns, ordered the family vault opened, written the obituary for *La Charente Libre* newspaper, and found the suit that Pierre would wear in the coffin. No one could rule out the possibility of suicide, not even Marie-France, who knew how vulnerable her kid brother was.

She had risen to the occasion. The funeral was beautiful and sumptuous. The priest praised the deceased, extolled his extraordinary sense of smell and "unwavering faith in the eau-de-vie of Charente," and commended him heartily to God and the saints. A limousine drove the rose-covered coffin to the Grand-Maisons cemetery, where the old Lavoisier vault shared the earth with the Lorrain and Mitterrand families.

Dying in May—how fitting, the insomniac thought as she poured herself some water from the small carafe on her night table. She drank a few sips and put the glass down next to a framed photograph of three children standing behind an enormous fish: a thirty-pound carp! Pierre had to be seven in this black-and-white photo. Claude-Henri was brandishing the carp from the end of his fishing pole. He looked like a triumphant pirate. At his right, the little girl with blonde curls was admiring her strong and handsome big brother. The three of them weren't far from the area where their grandfather's boat had allegedly gone down with the gold coins stashed below deck.

The heiress of Lavoisier Cognacs was dripping with fever. No, tonight she would not abandon herself to the bizarre blood moon that always sent peasants into turmoil. Everything people had said from time immemorial about this moon was nothing but rubbish. Marie-France knew it was not the scarlet rays of the moon that scorched the plants. Her grandfather had explained it to her.

"Things are both simpler and more complicated than that," he had said. "The light from the moon heats the atmosphere and evaporates the moisture that traps heat. This creates a risk of frost, even if the thermometer does not go below freezing. Do you understand?"

Marie-France had nodded, although she had not really grasped her grandfather's explanation.

In the photo, Pierre was wearing Bermuda shorts. His arms were stubbornly folded in front of his puny, shirtless chest, and his face was all dark eyes and sulking lips. The fish on display was repugnant to him. Pierre Lavoisier had always had an aversion to hunting and fishing. The idea of killing had been unbearable to him.

So how could he have had the courage to kill himself? Perhaps it was an accident, after all. But Pierre was a formidable swimmer. No one in Jarnac could do a better crawl stroke. And since childhood, Pierre had known the treacherous nature of the Charente—its deceitful currents, deadly whirlpools, and menacing embankments. No. Unless he had suffered a dizzy spell.

Certainly, the autopsy had revealed a minor contusion on his left temple, but nothing that would suggest a crime. Pierre Lavoisier had died of cold-water shock sometime after dinner, although there was no explanation of how or why he was in the water. The inquiry assigned to the Jarnac Police Department by the prosecutor from Angoulême had noted the unfortunate absence of any eyewitness or trauma on the victim's body, "except the hematoma on the skull's temporal cavity." Several Jarnac inhabitants had come forward to claim that the youngest Lavoisier had some reasons to take his life. But there was no hard evidence to support this.

Marie-France pulled the folds of her white robe around her tanned throat. She got up and went to the window. Under the red moon, the garden, with its willow-tree border, and the countryside beyond were a play of shadows and light. She threw open the window and wearily lit a cigarette. A cool breeze rushed into the room and slipped under her soft robe. Marie-France began to shiver. Other than the soft wind, there were no sounds at all—no bats swooshing in the air, no frogs or crickets in the grass. The night was perfectly silent.

A splash from the river broke the stillness. It sounded like a sack of cement being thrown into the water. Marie-France was unfazed and took another drag of her cigarette. The carp were dancing. Could it be mating season? She contemplated Little Pierre for a long moment and finally surrendered to the sofa. The red moon enveloped her until the weariness and cold sent her back to her bed. In three hours it would be day.

6

"I will fight until my last breath! Do you hear me, Mr. Cooker?"

"I hope so, and you can be sure, Ms. Lavoisier, that I will be at your side," Benjamin responded. He could see that Marie-France did not fully grasp his intentions.

The winemaker caught Virgile's smile. He also saw that Ms. Lavoisier was watching closely and most likely assessing the dynamic between him and his assistant. No doubt about it, she was a mature, self-possessed, and shrewd woman, quick to get back on her feet.

"Which means?" Marie-France asked.

"I have decided to give up this assignment entrusted to me by your minor shareholder," Benjamin said, slipping his Havana cigar into a groove of the green porcelain ashtray bearing the message "Settle for nothing but Lavoisier cognac."

"May I at least know the conclusions of your report?" she asked as she hastily signed the correspondence that her secretary was giving her, piece by piece.

"There will be no conclusions," Benjamin responded.

"I understand you are not a man to give up easily."

"This decision is a precedent in my career, but please don't ask me to explain myself."

"I don't mean to pry. I would simply like to apologize for your initial reception. You understand, at Lavoisier Cognacs, we are not in the habit of opening our books. Or our hearts, for that matter."

She threw out her chest and in doing so showed some cleavage. Benjamin imagined that underneath her dress, there was a black silk bustier pushing up her bosom. The woman's dark gaze fell on Virgile.

"My brother's death is pulling me further into the lion's den each day, but I haven't had my last word. I have friends in high places."

"You're going to need them, madam. You won't be surprised when I say that you will need both financial and moral support. You and your brother were very close, weren't you?" The winemaker had heard the rumors about Marie-France and her brother, but he knew this proud woman well enough to understand that she wouldn't respond to innuendo.

"Pierre was more than a brother," she said. "I could tell that the takeover threat was consuming him. He had become a different person. He was nervous, fearful, almost paranoid."

Marie-France picked up her pack of cigarettes and offered one to Virgile, never taking her eyes off him.

"Maybe later," Virgile said. He was looking self-conscious. Then, in the same breath, he blurted out, "Your brother did not commit suicide."

"How can you be so certain?" Marie-France asked. "I am full of doubt myself."

"I believe I was the last person to speak to Pierre before his death. Your brother was working on new ideas for the business. I was witness to his last blends. What marvels! There was fire in his eyes. No sign of depression. Pierre—I am calling him that because he asked me to—was incapable of killing himself. He loved life too much. Of course, he was affected by your other brother's sale of his shares, but Pierre had faith in you. He knew you were capable of preserving the Lavoisier honor. No, even the thought of suicide was against his nature."

"What are you getting at?" the heiress said, crushing her cigarette in the ashtray where Benjamin's cigar was slowly smoldering.

"I take it you are rejecting the accident theory?" Benjamin hastened to clarify.

"I have a hard time imagining Pierre falling into the river without managing to reach the bank," Marie-France said.

"Which means that you are convinced, just as we are, that your brother did not die a natural death," the winemaker summed up, looking at his assistant. He noticed that Virgile's shirttail was coming out of his jeans. The lapse annoyed him.

"Was anyone angry with your brother?" Virgile asked. "Did he keep company with any shady characters?"

"Shady? No, not at all," Marie-France said.

"If you don't mind, I'll take that cigarette," Virgile said.

"Oh, yes, of course."

"What I am asking is this: Who might have benefited from your brother's death?"

"I…I have no idea," Marie-France answered.

"Well, I have an idea," Virgile said. Now he seemed assured, almost impertinent.

"I can't think of anyone," Marie-France insisted. After a long silence she added, "Apart from the Asians, maybe, but that would be jumping to conclusions. Unless it has something to do with your recent decision to resign, Mr. Cooker."

"Integrity and ethics drove my decision to resign, madam, and I made up my mind before your brother's death. I waited to tell you about it until this morning."

"I admit I don't understand much anymore," Marie-France said just as she noticed that her pen was leaking. Her fingertips were turning black with ink, and color was rising in her cheeks.

"With all due respect, boss, there are two opposing theories if we start from the premise that Pierre Lavoisier's death is advantageous to a third party," Virgile said. "The crime could have been ordered by the Chinese, but one could also imagine that your older brother, Ms. Lavoisier, with the price he negotiated for his shares, might have had an interest in eliminating someone who held a little over thirty-three percent of the company."

"Young man, I will not allow you to accuse my brother!" Marie-France responded angrily as she searched for something to wipe her hand with. She motioned to her secretary to fetch a towel. "Obviously, Claude-Henri is at the root of all our troubles, but he's not a murderer."

Benjamin reached for his cigar, brought it to his lips, and took a deep puff before carefully putting it down again.

"Ms. Lavoisier, there are many people who were surprised, actually shocked, by your older brother's absence at Pierre's funeral. You must admit that his silence does not argue in his favor."

"Claude was not there because he did not know about Pierre's death. I can't tell you where he's hiding. I haven't heard from him since he left Jarnac. Not a phone call! Not a letter! I moved heaven and earth to find him. I published Pierre's death notice in *Le Figaro* and *Le Monde*. In vain. Up until the morning of the funeral, I hoped that he would find out, that he'd show up."

Marie-France was holding herself together. She was not a woman prone to tears. Again, she scrutinized Virgile. Was she jealous of his young assistant who had become so close to Pierre in the last hours of his life? Or was she coming on to him? Or was it both?

"When you left that night, what did he say to you, Mr. Lanssien? Did he seem anxious or preoccupied?"

Virgile was fiddling with the cigarette, which he hadn't lit. Benjamin knew that he hated blond tobacco.

"He was clearly happy when I left. He spent more than an hour showing me his herbarium and giving me a lecture on scents. I never could have..."

Virgile's cell phone rang inside his leather jacket. He stopped talking to take the call.

"Hello. Yes, Jacqueline, I will tell him right away. Okay, I will let him know."

Virgile turned to Benjamin. He was grinning. "Once again, boss, you turned off your cell phone, and the prime minister's office is trying to get hold of you! I just spoke to Jacqueline. She says it's very important. You need to call her right away."

Benjamin reached for his Lusitania and excused himself. He left Marie-France's office. Obviously, this business would require a certain amount of confidentiality.

§ § §

Virgile found himself alone with Pierre Lavoisier's sister. He walked over to the window, where he could survey the entire winery. The branches of a crepe myrtle were tapping against the glass. Marie-France followed him.

"May I ask you a personal question?" she said. "You spoke a lot with my brother in those last hours. He may have told you certain things, things that men talk about between themselves."

"I will answer if I can."

"Was there a woman in Pierre's life?"

"Yes," Virgile answered without hesitation. "And you know the answer. The woman was you."

§ § §

When Benjamin reappeared in the office, he noted that the conversation between his assistant and the director of Lavoisier Cognacs had taken on a decidedly more intimate tone.

"Virgile, I need to talk to you in private," he said. Benjamin left the office again, with Virgile on his heels.

"Our business is taking a turn that I do not care for, Virgile. I have a meeting at five thirty today in the Jarnac cemetery, at the tomb of you know who, with an envoy of the prime minister, a certain Antoine de Gaulejat. It concerns the family business. Obviously, this woman—who has her eyes on you—enjoys some protection. Here's a bit of advice: don't get too close, or you might get stung!"

"You're giving me that advice, sir? Which of us has been visiting a certain person's garden lately?"

"How do you know that, you rascal?"

"Cognac is a small town, sir."

"Don't get any ideas, Virgile. I'm a married man. Understand?" Benjamin gave his assistant a comradely pat on the back, as he did whenever a complicit agreement needed no words.

When the two men returned to the office, the heiress had slipped away, leaving a card that read: "We all have our secrets, M.F."

7

In the dying light of day, an army of wind- and rain-battered crosses rose up amid rows of forgotten tombs. The same Charente stone that had been used for these grave markers and tombs had gone into the most beautiful wine cellars in Saintonge. On this afternoon, the west wind hadn't diminished the warmth of the sun or the heady springtime scents. Benjamin stepped up his pace. He knew he was late.

The thickset stranger was standing at the entrance of the Grand-Maisons cemetery, under the shelter where the deceased occupants of the various plots were listed on a map. The emissary didn't appear to be interested in the map or its fastidious directory of plots. He was wearing a dark green coat, a matching scarf, and a broad-brimmed black fedora. As Benjamin drew closer, he saw him checking his watch—his time was undoubtedly precious—and pushing his tortoise-shell glasses up his aquiline nose.

When the man spotted Benjamin, he started walking toward him. The winemaker noticed that he had a slight limp. His age was indeterminate, and his complexion was sallow. He approached Benjamin with the unctuous smile of public servants who had spent a long time in the Government Accountability Office or the Council of State before joining the minister's personal staff. There was cunning in his bright eyes and charm, too. When they greeted, Benjamin noted the smooth tone of his voice. It was the voice of someone who wasn't one to give orders, but instead, one who persuaded others, mostly on behalf of high-level and nebulous interests.

The two men started walking along the paths snaking through the cemetery, which took them on a sort of pilgrimage from one section to another. They meandered among the recently interred and then turned left to venture closer to the chapels and mausoleums that stood testament to the fortunes of those who had died long ago. The gates were rusty, and the inscriptions were covered with lichen. The virgins of Lourdes and cherubs wore vexed expressions, but here the dead were cloaked in antiquated dignity, which Benjamin deemed fitting. As they walked, the emissary punctuated his remarks with "Isn't that so," and Benjamin responded with nods.

They slowed down, and the man spoke in an even lower voice. "The government is following this situation closely and looks unfavorably on any Chinese takeover of the Lavoisier business. The finance minister has been charged with handling the matter, and the prime minister has given instructions to prevent any transaction that might not go in the direction of..."

"I knew Ms. Lavoisier had influence," Benjamin said. He felt his blood pressure rising. Marie-France had said she had friends, but he never suspected that she had friends who were this important. He searched his pockets for a Havana and then thought better of it. Smoking a cigar in this place would be sacrilege. He controlled the urge and instead nervously rubbed his fingers together.

"It's less about the interests of the person who brings us together and more about what her cognacs represent," the emissary said as he narrowed his eyes. "Her cognacs are intrinsically French and part of our heritage." Benjamin detected a cunning tone in his voice.

"Don't be offended if I don't believe you," the winemaker responded.

"That's your prerogative," the emissary said just as curtly.

The man stopped in front of a chapel guarded by two Florentine cypress trees. The one on the left was taller than its counterpart. "You see, Mr. Cooker, the health of this conifer symbolizes the valiant ideas upheld by the man buried here in 1996."

"That, Mr. Gaulejat, depends on whose side you are on. You see, this taller cypress is to our left, but you must agree that it is to the right of François Mitterand, the deceased president you mean to honor."

The prime minister's emissary smiled and lowered his head as if to pay his respects.

"Come, Mr. Cooker, you've been hired by the Chinese to organize in a perfectly orthodox manner what amounts to a takeover bid. Is that not so?"

"My assignment was of a different nature—"

"Why are you talking about it in the past tense? Have you ended your relationship?"

"In a way."

"I understand that the methods employed by your clients might shock you, Mr. Cooker."

"What are you getting at?"

"The death of Ms. Lavoisier's brother is a bit surprising, is it not?"

"I have questions regarding his death, just as everyone else does."

"You are not a man who would deny the obvious. I believe you owe your fame to your ability to clearly express your convictions regarding grand and petit crus. In fact, that's your business, is it not? Surely you know that this affair is turning to vinegar. That's characteristic of bad wine, isn't it?"

Taciturn now, Benjamin Cooker made an about-face and went to sit on a stone bench flanked by two chapels, where gaudy silk flowers filled the vases. The man followed, extending his bum leg as he sat down and wearily untying his scarf. Benjamin couldn't avoid smelling the man's rank breath.

The winemaker observed this man with a coolness inherited from his father, which some people mistook for arrogance.

"Mr. Gaulejat, if you are so certain, you must be privy to information that I don't have. To tell the truth, we are not in the same business. I don't intend to interfere with your business. I would hope you feel the same way."

"Far be it from me to offend you!"

"You are not offending me. But if I had any idea that I'd become embroiled in such mysterious conspiracies over work a Chinese company hired me to perform, I would have thought twice."

"You already have thought twice, since you tell me that you're dropping this assignment."

"For my own reasons."

"I am not interested in your reasons. I am sure they are good. But it is up to you to discourage Mr. Cheng's attempts. Lavoisier is a French product and must remain so. I don't have much else to say to you."

The emissary rose from the bench. He grimaced. His leg was obviously hurting.

"My dear friend, tell your Chinese representatives that the French government does not appreciate the elimination of Pierre Lavoisier," the man said. "Any persistence on their part will result in an official investigation, which would inevitably have unpleasant consequences. Really, Mr. Cooker, you are a smart man. Your decision proves it. We only ask you to use your powers of persuasion."

Smiling, the prime minister's emissary was tipping his fedora when Benjamin spoke up. "Mr. Gaulejat, how do you know Claude-Henri did not kill his brother?"

"The same way you do, Mr. Cooker. Family loyalties run deep."

The man took his leave. His foot scraped the gravel path as he walked away, which made Benjamin think of Talleyrand, the crafty eighteenth-century diplomat. Then his silhouette disappeared between two gravestones. A few minutes later, the gate of the Grands-Maisons cemetery groaned in the setting sun.

Benjamin walked over to the chapel with the two cypress trees, which were responding to the wind's commands. A couple with a child in tow stopped between the graves of General Pierre Quantin and politician-dramatist Ludovic Vitet. The woman turned to her husband. "See that? No one even decorates their graves anymore!"

When her husband did not reply, she persisted. "The French have a short memory."

Benjamin decided it was finally time to light his Cohiba. At this hour of the day, who cared about good manners? But the wind had picked up, and his lighter wasn't working. He ducked into a tiny alcove in the chapel. The smell of mildew made him sneeze.

Now sheltered from the wind, the winemaker succeeded in getting a flame. It illuminated two dates: 1916 and 1996. He lit his Havana with the pleasure of a pyromaniac. The cigar emitted strange odors of humus and undergrowth. If it had been a month earlier and dark already, it would have looked like a will-o'-the-wisp. Benjamin left the chapel and strolled through the cemetery until a public employee brandishing a bunch of keys shouted, "We're closing, mister!"

§ § §

Pierre Lavoisier had lived in the Château Floyras's old greenhouse. Fifteen years earlier he had transformed the building, which was overflowing with light, into a Baroque cabinet of curios. Red velvet drapes kept the ravaging rays of the sun from fading the rugs and paintings in his carefully managed disorder. Despite the clutter, the space smelled clean and fresh, because Pierre had planted lemon trees in oversized wooden crates, which he put here and there throughout the greenhouse. From his makeshift home, Pierre could see the waters of the Charente flowing at the back of the garden, between the alders and willow trees.

The cushions and sofas were meant to welcome visitors. But this amateur painter, part-time antiquarian, occasional gardener, and most assuredly collector of emotions and curiosities never entertained anyone. According to Marie-France, Pierre shut himself up for days and nights in his solitary retreat, lighting chandeliers and candelabras whose smoke blackened the ceilings. Shortly before his death, he had set aside his painting and reading and had spent practically all of his time sniffing—sniffing and inhaling scents from his albums of dried plants and his collection of vials. He had been on a quest to awaken what he called "the lost scents."

The very day of his death, he had shown Virgile his great herbarium and explained the dozens of plants and their faded odors: fireweed, evening primrose, great burnet, stitchwort, mignonette, delphinium, and Adonis, whose flower had lost its purple color but still had a lingering scent of brown sugar.

Virgile had participated fully, plunging his nose into the pages, where Latin names were mixed with contemporary terms. "Smell this! Yes, you are right. It smells like aniseed. But it also has a faint scent of grilled almonds, don't you think?"

And then Pierre would bend over another dried flower and compare the preserved scent with the aroma in one of the vials. "It's a rare smell that you find in certain wines from the Rhône Valley, near Condrieu."

Pierre's gestures were fresh in Virgile's mind, and he remembered how his voice took on a more serious tone whenever he was perplexed by an indefinable bouquet. He seemed to be still there, in his greenhouse, about to emerge from behind the antique Japanese screen or the purple drape surrounding his four-poster bed.

Why had Marie-France brought him to the greenhouse? "Come," she had said simply, as if she didn't have the courage to face her brother's fanciful world alone. "Pierre was different—"

Virgile felt awkward, at a loss for words, but he tried hard not to lose his composure in Pierre's sumptuous mess. His ran his finger over a geode, and then he weighed it in his hand.

"You know, Pierre never allowed me to come here," Marie-France said. "He cultivated the art of secrecy."

"Yet you assured Mr. Cooker that you had searched his desk to make sure he hadn't changed his will or written a letter before—"

"I lied."

"Why?"

"Probably because I didn't want to face reality."

"What reality?"

"We were so close, my brother and I, but at odds in our ambitions and passions. We only talked about things we had in common. Apart from that—"

Marie-France picked up a brass candlesnuffer and started digging out the blackened wax.

"Apart from that, silence was the best course," she said.

Flanked by a Moroccan brass lamp and a huge philodendron, Pierre's mahogany roll-top desk sat in a corner of the greenhouse. Above the desk was an enamel sign. "Cognac Lavoisier: Of course you deserve it!" The desk was embellished with a marble slab on which Pierre had arranged various navigational instruments, all shiny and certainly in perfect working condition. There was a large sextant, a small boat compass with an alidade, a telescope, a bronze ship's bell, and miniature Levasseur and Delagrave maps. The mail slots held old letters and postcards. A green leather blotter gave a final touch of elegance to this desk, swept clear of all paperwork. Virgile presumed that Pierre kept his papers in the desk drawers, all three of which were locked. Life in this little corner of his greenhouse world was in perfect order: tidy, arranged, shiny.

"If your brother wanted to take his life, he would have explained why in a letter, and he would have left it in clear view on his desk—under this geode, for example. You can be sure of that."

"You're right." Marie-France sighed as she dropped into a club chair. She poked her fingernail in the cigarette burns on the armrests. Her agitation seemed somewhat pathetic to Virgile.

"So you haven't tried to find out anything by going through his personal things?"

"No, all I did was open his last bank statement."

"And?"

"It's strange. Pierre was overdrawn. That wasn't like him. He was writing a lot of checks."

"His passion for antiques, maybe?" Virgile asked.

"Maybe." She gazed at all the furniture, the paintings, and the knickknacks patiently accumulated since childhood. Virgile wondered if she knew the significance of the objects that filled this greenhouse, or were they just things to her?

"Who might have been angry with your brother?"

"I don't know, unless it was—"

"Yes, I know, the Chinese investors. But it's too easy to make them the villains in this."

The Lavoisier Cognacs heiress had succeeded in working her fingernail through one of the burn marks. Now she was ripping the leather and digging into the cotton and horsehair padding beneath it.

"You say your brother had drained his bank account. Do you know where his money was going?"

Marie-France was quiet. She seemed to be staring at the Charente River shimmering in the distance. A shaft of light from the door, which had been left ajar, was making its way into the greenhouse.

Virgile started to inspect the desk more closely, and he motioned to Marie-France to join him.

"No, please, search it yourself, Mr. Lanssien. I can't bring myself to do it."

She extracted her fingers from the interior of the armrests, and the smell of old cigarettes wafted through the room. She got up and found the key to the drawers.

Meticulously and almost deferentially, Benjamin Cooker's assistant opened each of the three drawers. The first contained an album of black-and-white photos, some negatives in an envelope labeled "Martin Lamour," and art photos and portraits taken in Saintes, along with a few sketches of a rather handsome man. The second drawer held an old address book and an insurance policy listing all the furnishings and valuable objects in the greenhouse. The third drawer contained bank statements from Crédit Agricole Charente Périgord in carefully annotated folders. A dozen checkbook registers accounted for all of Pierre Lavoisier's expenses. For the most part, and especially for the oldest ones, nothing was missing: dates, names of recipients, purpose of the expenditures, or exact amounts. The registers went back more than five years.

Finances really weren't Virgile's strong suit. He treated his own checking account with a certain casual attitude, and this cost him substantial over-draft fees every month. But now he was method-ically going over Pierre's figures and annotations. And at the end of his examination, he had found that the recipient and the purpose of some of the transactions were missing. In each case the amount was considerable, and the handwriting looked shaky. Virgile gave his findings to Marie-France, who had sat down again in the leather chair.

"You can see why he was overdrawn," Virgile said.

"Maybe he was buying antiques at auction and was just too preoccupied to pay attention to his bookkeeping," Marie-France suggested.

"I don't think so. Each time your brother bought a piece of furniture or a painting, he recorded the amount and the name of the auctioneer, as well as what it was that he bought. You can see that on every check stub. No, I think that—"

"You think what?" Marie-France asked. She was avoiding eye contact.

"That these expenses weren't very—let's say—orthodox."

"Meaning?"

"Perhaps there was someone in your brother's life, and he was keeping it a secret from you."

"A love life I knew nothing about?"

"Yes, it's not all that unusual for a man to hide an affair. Your brother may have had his reasons, and you said yourself that you never came to his greenhouse. How would you know if he didn't tell you?"

Marie-France had lit a cigarette and was making fresh burns in the leather upholstery. She seemed to be taking pleasure in this, and the greenhouse was beginning to smell like singed fabric.

"Pierre was a very discreet man."

"Okay, but was he the type to pay a call girl when he went to Paris or traveled to some other city?"

"Pierre hardly ever left Jarnac."

"So you don't know of any guilty pleasures he might have had?"

"I don't know what you are referring to."

"You couldn't have lived next door to your brother and not have known anything about his weaknesses or his social life, Ms. Lavoisier. Either you know things you don't want to reveal for reasons you haven't shared with me, which makes your brother's death even more suspicious and you a potential suspect, or else Pierre was a mystery to you, in which case his death is all the more puzzling. In either case, allow me to quote my boss. 'When suspicion sets in, let's not run away!'"

Marie-France Lavoisier crushed out the cigarette and smoothed her blouse. She walked over to the desk where Virgile was going through the payouts that had no designated recipients. Virgile felt a little like a schoolboy toiling over his homework. He had never been good at math, and all the figures were making him dizzy.

"I wish I could help you, Mr. Lanssien."

He felt two hands on his shoulders. Long fingers were exploring his deltoids and rising with exquisite slowness to his neck. The odor of patchouli accompanied this sensual assault, and heavy breathing caressed him behind his ear. Virgile did not turn around. Now an expert hand was stroking his chest, brushing his nipples, and sliding toward his belly.

Virgile leaned back and closed his eyes. The words on the sign ran through his head. "Cognac Lavoisier: Of course you deserve it!"

8

Benjamin Cooker was late for his noon meeting on the patio of the Ritz at the Place Vendômc. He had driven all the way to Paris for the appointment, but he knew his punctual client, Shiyi Cheng, would be offended if he was even ten minutes late. Benjamin could see the businessman, alone, eyeing the nearby tables as he impatiently fiddled with his glass of Moët et Chandon. No doubt, he was envious of the lucrative deals being brokered all around him.

The winemaker didn't trust his client's unctuous smile. He knew this kind of man's manners all too well and detected anger in Cheng's pinched lips. Benjamin feigned the attitude of a busy man dispensing with formalities. He was tempted to refuse the glass of Champagne, but his good manners prevailed. In a tone both courteous and artful, he informed Cheng of his intention to cut his assignment short. He would not be completing the Lavoisier audit.

"At any rate, the French finance minister will use every means at his disposal to prevent a change of hands. I was approached by one of the prime minister's advisors to inform you of the government's position on this matter, which is considered sensitive for reasons I am not at liberty to explain."

"This is not exactly what we were expecting from you, Mr. Cooker. We were hoping to have an expert's opinion. You accepted the assignment, and we agreed on your fee. You will need to complete the task."

Benjamin slid his right hand inside his jacket and pulled out his checkbook. He opened it.

"What are you doing, Mr. Cooker?"

"As you can see, I am reimbursing you for the entire amount I received. I believe we are even now. I thank you for your confidence, and I am truly sorry that I am unable to honor my commitment."

The man put down his glass and angrily tore up the check.

"You are on Ms. Lavoisier's payroll. You disappoint me, Mr. Cooker!"

"I am beholden to no one. I am simply disengaging myself."

"That's not the way it works," Cheng said, pinching his thin lips even tighter. "You misunderstand our intentions. We are not attempting to impose our influence over anyone. Do, however, tell Ms. Lavoisier that the unfortunate death of her younger brother may just change the balance of power."

"I certainly will," Benjamin answered curtly. "And while we're at it, here's my own piece of information: the public prosecutor of Angoulême is ready to open an investigation of Pierre Lavoisier's death. Indeed, there are many questions. I think you could be in the prosecutor's crosshairs."

"What are you suggesting?"

"I've simply passed along what I've learned," Benjamin replied.

"My dear friend, you should put your mind to better use. For example, has your close associate, young Lanssien, told you anything about the true nature of the man who was fished out of the Charente River? They even say that..."

Cheng's cell phone rang. "I beg you to excuse me. I am expecting an important call."

The man stood up to take the call, walked into the lobby of the luxury hotel, and disappeared behind a pink marble column. When he returned, the minority shareholder of Lavoisier Cognacs didn't seem to be at all concerned about Benjamin's resignation. In fact, he looked jubilant. He asked Benjamin to have another glass of Champagne. The winemaker refused and quickly said good-bye, but not before Cheng could get in a parting shot.

"Mr. Cooker, choose your sides carefully," he said. "Think about it another day or two. In Jarnac, the waters of the Charente are murky and deep. You can't see what's lurking beneath the surface."

"Good day, Mr. Cheng, and now I have a metaphor for you. As Jean de la Fontaine put it: never sell the skin of a bear that you haven't caught."

The Place Vendôme was radiant under the Parisian sky when Benjamin left the hotel. A shower had washed the pavement clean and chased the tourists away from the jewelry store windows. Benjamin felt surprisingly carefree. Tomorrow he would be back at Grangebelle, at Elisabeth's side. In the Médoc, the grapevines would be flowering, and soon there would be the first growth. No, before that, he would drive back to Jarnac, pick up the incorrigible Virgile, and have a frank discussion with the Lavoisier woman. Maybe he would even make a detour to Samson's Mill to see Sheila Scott and her roses. For one last good-bye.

§ § §

The dusty dining room at Château Floyras didn't appear to be used very often, if at all. The light from the lone crystal chandelier barely illuminated the embroidered tablecloth. Portraits on the toile-papered walls displayed the Lavoisier line like an ancient family album. All had hooked noses and thick eyebrows and wore solemn expressions. A French-Egyptian Revival–style sideboard and a Dutch wood-burning stove were the only furnishings, other than the table and chairs.

Benjamin had been unable to refuse the invitation. The mistress of the house had insisted that he attend dinner. Naturally, Virgile was among the guests, as was a certain Maurice Fauret de Solmilhac, a braggart who, with ancestors from Périgord, had a touch of Gascony in his accent. He had a mischievous look and an obvious propensity for womanizing. Mr. Gaulejat, the special envoy, and he could have been twins, Benjamin thought. Solmilhac was a dapper man in his sixties with thick silver hair combed back and light blue eyes. He was wearing a signet ring that displayed a coat of arms and a Prince of Wales jacket with a blue silk handkerchief that matched his eyes. He was a confirmed bachelor and a longtime friend of the Lavoisier family, there for them in hard times and ready to put himself on the line to win the favors of the beautiful Marie-France. There was no doubt that he would boot the Chinese out of Jarnac for her. Moreover, his intentions were clear, as were the scowls he aimed at Virgile.

"You are lucky, young man, to be rubbing elbows at your age with an authority on wine, the most famous one in France, no less—Europe for that matter and even the world," he told Virgile.

"Very lucky, indeed, sir, which, believe me, I am more aware of every day," Virgile replied.

Benjamin was not talkative. The duck was too dry. The potatoes were a bit too brown, and the Burgundy aligote was so-so. There was nothing at all appealing about this dinner. The conversation, meanwhile, was spiritless, despite Marie-France's attempts to orchestrate a convivial atmosphere. Benjamin refused to do his bit, and Virgile's pitiful attempts at conversation weren't enough to compensate. Finally, Benjamin decided to glean something worthwhile from the forced gathering. He turned to Fauret de Solmilhac.

"You seem to know everything about me. You've read my guides and drunk many of my wines. I, on the other hand, know nothing about you, Mr. Fauret de Solmilhac, other than the fact that you are a tireless friend of our hostess."

"Would you like to know my background? Actually, it's not very interesting. Let's say I do some brokering, which, thank heavens, has been rather profitable. I was a lawyer in Paris before that. The cases I witnessed in the courtrooms back then had the makings of great theater."

The man had raised his voice as if to demonstrate that he was a talented speaker, even something of an orator.

"You might say my real profession today is lobbying. I have certain interpersonal skills, if you know what I mean."

"I can see that very well," the winemaker said, dabbing his napkin on his lips.

"I might add that you know the whole planet!" Marie-France said with affected enthusiasm.

"The entire world? That's going a bit too far, my dear Marie. Just a few influential people, which is enough to make me happy."

"You are a happy man, then," Virgile said. Benjamin picked up the derisive tone in his assistant's voice. But he didn't think their dinner companions knew Virgile well enough to discern it.

"In business, I believe I can reply in the affirmative, young man."

"And in love?" Virgile asked. Benjamin noted the presumptuous smile.

"In that area, you have to be young, my boy, to believe in happiness."

Sensing the coming storm, Benjamin switched to a 1994 Beau-Séjour-Bécot much more to his liking and said, "Happiness engulfs our strength, just as misfortune extinguishes our virtues."

"François-René de Chateaubriand suits you well, Mr. Cooker," the businessman said.

"May I suggest that you give credit—without interest, mind you—to Balzac, rather than Chateaubriand? Words and keen insight into the human heart were these writers' real treasures.

Both were penniless when the trumpets of fame began to sound."

"I know, I know," the man replied. Benjamin could see that he was not someone who allowed himself to be shown up. "So, Mr. Cooker, what do you think of this Saint-Émilion?"

"Quite good, perhaps even better than good," the winemaker responded laconically.

"Say there, Marie-France, why are you being so quiet?" Solmilhac said, turning to their hostess. "And just when I have some news to share. You don't need to add the fear of losing your cognacs to your troubles. I have found Claude-Henri. He's in Canada. I think I can convince him to sell me his shares at a higher price than that scoundrel Cheng. Let me handle it. You know how important your company's independence is to me."

The man wrapped his hand around Marie-France's wrist and gave it a squeeze. Marie-France was playing along. Benjamin had already surmised that there was something between Marie-France and his assistant, and even though he made it a point to avoid prying into Virgile's private affairs, he guessed that the young man had experience with mature women. He watched as Virgile smiled and checked his watch. Benjamin suppressed a yawn. The dinner had been frightfully dull, and this Fauret de Solmilhac was insufferably smug. It was time to end the ordeal.

He had no intention of lighting his Havana and lingering even a few minutes more.

"No cigar, Mr. Cooker? You must have one with a '55 Lavoisier. Wouldn't you agree?" Marie-France was insistent.

"I don't think I deserve it tonight."

"Why do you say that?"

"I think the one who truly deserves your fine cognac—and credit—is your friend here, who intends to free you from the clutches of your foreign shareholders."

"But I must tell you that your decision to end your alliance with the Asians allows me to look to the future with greater confidence."

"May I suggest, Ms. Lavoisier, that you exercise the greatest caution?"

"But the government is against a Chinese acquisition," said the lawyer-turned-businessman.

"Certainly, certainly. Yet you know as well as I that there is a fine art to finding the right blend," Benjamin said, looking directly at Marie-France.

The winemaker and his assistant finally accepted just a few drops of cognac in their coffee. Benjamin sniffed the old eau-de-vie and admired the scents of sandalwood, lychee, and passion fruit.

"Mr. Cooker, let's give time the time it needs," Solmihlac said.

Marie-France offered more cognac.

Benjamin and Virgile politely declined. Fauret de Solmilhac held out his glass. He was staying at the château, after all, and didn't need to worry about driving. Benjamin was dying to get back to the hotel without any more incidents involving the keystone cops. The previous week's ticket and fine were sufficient reasons to decline any more alcohol.

Benjamin watched his assistant as Marie-France, the seductress, slipped away in favor of national and family interest. She had luxuriated in having two lovers at her table. In this area, as in so many others, she excelled. Benjamin didn't know if his young assistant, vulnerable despite all his worldliness, would ever forgive her.

9

The next day, Benjamin meandered through the beds of Gallica rosebushes with the curiosity of a botanist ready to delight in each and every specimen. Over there was the Belle de Crécy, with its thorns, alongside the Duchess of Angoulême and the Belle Éveque dressed in purple. He admired the perfect Ombre and the exquisite Tricolore de Flandres and then, farther on, over the little Japanese bridge, the Alba roses, vigorous and rustic and never more beautiful than in June. On this spring morning, the rosebuds were giving off a musky scent under black clouds racing across the sky and squadrons of swallows excited by the ocean winds.

Benjamin focused on each flower as Sheila dazzled him with her ability to name the varieties planted over the years since her writer companion, Styron, had ended his life for reasons never clearly understood.

Sheila Scott was already talking about the flowers to come, the ones that would take root there, in the shade of the linden tree, and those that would soon climb the trellises, not to mention the tea roses, the ones from China, their double flowers so lovely in shape and color. Here was a King of Siam, there a Triomphe du Luxembourg. The Englishwoman talked and talked. She seemed to be trying to keep her visitor at any price. Sheila dreaded saying good-bye. Although Benjamin was showing no eagerness to leave, the idea that her friend, her first love, might soon run off was unbearable.

"May I offer you a cup of tea? I bought some Grand Yunnan. Don't tell me you don't have time!"

"How could I refuse?"

"So? Where are you with your assignment?"

"Finished."

"Already?"

"Not that it ever really began."

"What do you mean? You have a way of being so secretive, and I found it exasperating at the École des Beaux-Arts. Why can't you simply say what's on your mind?"

"Because with the Lavoisiers, nothing is simple, and the Chinese are not exactly extroverts. Under those conditions, how can anything be clear?"

For the occasion, Sheila had taken out her porcelain English teapot with a fanciful motif. She delicately lifted the lid and announced that the tea was not ready.

"She's going to be devoured by them before you know it," Sheila said as she set out a small dish of chocolate cookies.

"Maybe not."

"Are you really so naïve, Benjamin?"

"One of Marie-France's friends purportedly has convinced the Judas brother to sell him the shares he inherited when Pierre died."

"Oh, they found him?"

"Evidently. He is living in Montreal, and he's been investing in real estate."

"But the Asians will double their offer, and since that guy lives only for money, he won't be able to resist very long."

Sheila's English accent was more pronounced in the company of her compatriot. Benjamin thought it created a certain intimacy between them.

"The man says he will vouch for the deal, which is somewhat risky for Ms. Lavoisier, because she will be indebted to him when it comes to controlling the company," Benjamin said. He pointed to the teapot and asked Sheila to check it again.

"If he's a good match and a bachelor with some manners, all she has to do is marry him. It's as easy as that!"

"I think he is more or less all of those things," Benjamin said, amused by his friend's pragmatism and logic.

"Do you know his name? Maybe I know him."

"Maurice Fauret de Solmilhac, if I remember correctly."

Sheila, who had been about to pour the tea, stopped and looked at Benjamin. Her face darkened. Then she began to shake with laughter and spilled the tea on her jeans.

"Maurice! That bloody Maurice! That idiot Maurice! That bastard Maurice!"

"Obviously, you know him well. You do have secrets, don't you?" Benjamin said, pleased that Sheila's opinion confirmed what he himself thought of this lawyer has-been. He was also hoping to find out more about the mystery man he'd seen on his first visit to Samson's Mill.

"Do I know him? You, I can tell. He was my lover for a time when I first arrived in Migron. Oh, he's a charmer. Good looking for his age, too."

"Good speaker," Benjamin added as he poured his tea.

"A better speaker than lover! I can guarantee that. He's a disaster in bed."

"That could be a serious obstacle to any marriage with Ms. Lavoisier, at least from what I've heard," Benjamin said, hoping to get more details.

"He's a scoundrel. I lived with him for several months without ever knowing where his money was coming from. He was involved in politics and played every angle. I think he took bribes from businesses that were looking for government contracts. He used his influence with the right officials. This is a man who's involved in shenanigans and always has a beautiful woman on his arm. I can't believe your Lavoisier woman would be taken in by such an asshole. But then again, I was too. Maurice Fauret de Solmilhac! Him, a Lavoisier shareholder? What a nightmare!"

"I guess you would know," Benjamin said.

"Benjamin, you are not in the pocket of those investors anymore, and if you have any regard for that Lavoisier woman, whom I've never met, warn her, please."

"How could you have fallen for anyone so—"

"I was vulnerable. It was a few months after Styron's suicide. I had just arrived here, and I didn't know anyone. I was drifting. Alone."

The tea had cooled, but Sheila kept on adding sugar and sipping her Yunnan. Benjamin stood up and brushed the cookie crumbs off his pants.

"I must take my leave now. I have to meet Virgile."

"Virgile?"

"Yes, he's my assistant. I have become quite fond of him. I guess I consider him an adopted son now, if you know what I mean."

Sheila lowered her head. "But it's already noon. Why don't you stay for lunch?"

"It wouldn't look good. And I do need to see Virgile."

"Invite him. I'm dying to meet this young man you're so attached to."

"He doesn't have a car to get to Migron."

"Well, you could send him in a taxi. I remember you were a bit stingy back when you were a student. But I know you allow yourself a few extravagances these days."

"Fine, then!" Benjamin entered Virgile's number on his cell phone. "Oh, good heavens, I have no phone service!"

"Use the house phone. On the table inside."

Benjamin reached his assistant on the landline. As he made the call, he glanced at Sheila. She looked wistful. A bit nervous, too.

"I guess I'll just make myself at home until Virgile arrives," he said. As he hung up he spotted a flask on a nearby table. It had no label, just a piece of tape that read: "Sample for Nathan, 1979."

"Of course, Benjamin. You are at home here."

No sooner had she said this than the door banged open. A powerful gust of wind swooped into the front room and blew everything off the table. The dishes and teapot went flying and crashed to the floor. Outside, golf-ball-sized hail was assaulting the plants. The ground was already strewn with broken branches.

"Oh my God!" Sheila seemed petrified as she stared at the end-of-the-world spectacle through the window. Benjamin felt her edging closer. Her hand brushed his. He pulled it away but then looked at her face. She was holding back tears. Benjamin could no longer contain his feelings.

He took the rose grower of Samson's Mill into his arms. And on the radio in the kitchen, tuned to a golden oldies station, he heard Elton John: "Don't Go Breaking My Heart."

10

Lunch was a simple affair but quite congenial. Too congenial for Benjamin's taste. He did not care for Virgile's overly familiar attention to the woman who was blowing on the embers of their past love. Sheila had no qualms about revealing their former relationship. She even supplied details that did not show Benjamin in the best light. But the winemaker, with the help of the pineau, couldn't help smiling. It wasn't long before Virgile was taking the beautiful English woman's side as she gently teased him. Yes, he'd reprimand Virgile on the ride back, but that could wait.

Sheila praised Virgile's sense of humor, intelligence, wit, and charm as Benjamin and she sipped their coffee and Virgile inspected the garden.

"Don't overdo it, Sheila. He might fall for you. I know what he's capable of," Benjamin said, carefully removing the ring from the Cohiba he was planning to light.

They watched Virgile, the well-educated son of a farmer, examine the damage done by the hail and tend to the wounded vegetation. He straightened a bruised stalk and propped it against a stake. Farther on, he found a pair of pruning shears and snipped off a few branches broken by the onslaught.

"How old is your Virgile?" Sheila asked.

"He's barely thirty."

"Sociable?"

"The ladies find him attractive. Men seem to like him too. He has a weakness for women of a certain age, but I fear he is more vulnerable than he makes out to be."

He walked into the entry to take his Loden off the hook. He was in a hurry to say good-bye to the mercurial Marie-France.

"Is she prettier than me?"

"Younger, perhaps, but just as naughty."

"Benjamin, I forbid you to—"

"Sheila, you've always been a free spirit," he said, teasing her.

The winemaker stopped talking when Virgile appeared in the doorway. His assistant had gathered an armful of broken flowers.

"The hail and wind got to these," he told Sheila. "They were going to die anyway, so I thought you might enjoy them inside." He was the image of innocence and kindness.

Sheila thanked him profusely and even hugged him with affection.

Driving to Jarnac, Benjamin was quiet while Virgile hummed the last refrain of a Cunnie Williams R&B song.

"She's a very attractive woman, your Sheila. I bet she was a knockout when you two were in school."

"What are you trying to say, Virgile?"

"Nothing, boss. She could be my mom."

"I know you too well, my boy!"

"Are you jealous?"

"Don't push it, Virgile, please."

"I have the feeling I'm about to get myself in trouble."

"You already have." Benjamin slid a CD into the player to put an end to the conversation. The overture of *Véronique*, André Messager's operetta, lightened the atmosphere. Still, the two men ignored each other all the way to Jarnac. Virgile admired the landscape, while Benjamin grumbled.

§ § §

Marie-France Lavoisier tried to lead Virgile to the greenhouse. There was a present waiting for him, she whispered. Virgile declined the invitation. He looked blankly at the cognac heiress and simply shook her hand, saying sardonically, "We'll meet again one day, I'm sure." Benjamin guessed it was his way of letting her know he was done with Charente ways. Virgile would never understand them. Benjamin was hardly friendlier but impeccably courteous when he said his good-byes at Château Floyras. He said he looked forward to seeing her soon.

"Give my regards to Mr. Fauret de Solmilhac!" he told Marie-France, who stood transfixed on the front steps of the decadent neo-Renaissance-style mansion.

"I certainly will. He's sorry he couldn't be here to say good-bye."

"I'm sure," the winemaker replied as he revved the engine of his Mercedes convertible.

"So is that it?" Virgile asked as Benjamin eased into traffic on the N10, heading back to Bordeaux.

"Is what it?"

"We just leave Marie-France to that slimy Ferret dude because he's French and not Chinese? And what about Pierre? Do you really believe it was an accident?"

Benjamin chose not to say anything, only a laconic "Give time the time it needs. That's—"

"I know, I know: François Mitterand," Virgile spat out, giving Benjamin a look that verged on disdain.

Benjamin remained silent for a good twenty minutes, and then said, "Pierre's death may remain as much a mystery as his life was, but I think I can do something for the future of cognac."

§ § §

Benjamin Cooker celebrated being back home at Grangebelle by taking Elisabeth out to dinner and going for a long walk the next morning with his dog, Bacchus. Returning from the walk, he dressed for work and drove to his offices on the Allées de Tourny.

Cooker & Co. was known for its decorum. But Benjamin's secretary, Jacqueline Delmas, paid it no mind when it came to Virgile. Benjamin was thinking this when he heard his assistant waltz into the reception area. He didn't have to hear anything to know she was planting kisses on Virgile's cheeks. This was her way of greeting him.

"You are like sunshine!" she would tell him.

And invariably Virgile would reply, "For someone who brings good weather, I'm not paid enough."

To which Jacqueline would say in a hushed voice, "You should ask Mr. Cooker for a little raise." On this day she added two lines. "But you'll have to wait. He's been spending an inordinate amount of time on the phone this morning."

"Who with?"

"I don't know," Jacqueline said. "He's been very hush-hush about it."

"Whatever," Virgile replied. "Do you know if Alexandrine is in the lab?"

§ § §

It was mating season. The frogs had been copulating all night, offering a concert of croaking loud enough to keep an entire regiment awake. The inexpensive bed-and-breakfast had a lumpy bed and windows so thin, Virgile felt like he was right in the middle of a theater of amorous frolicking. The muggy night heralded a sweltering summer. It was only at the first light of dawn that Virgile finally fell asleep. Now he was lying there, thinking about what had brought him back to Jarnac: Sheila.

At that lunch, he had barely noticed the picture and had forgotten it when he cleaned up the garden, but now it was haunting him. He had to see it again. He'd wheedled the lab's small van out of Alexandrine de la Palussière, who always claimed that she needed it to get to the vineyards in Haut-Brion or Pape Clément. She made him promise to have it back the next day. Then he'd called Sheila and played his charm card. Now she was expecting him for breakfast—and perhaps a little more, he feared.

He drove up the drive lined with hazelnut trees and noticed that Samson's rose grower had pulled back the curtains and thrown open the kitchen window. When he parked the van, he breathed in the scent of wild mint from the river and the aroma of coffee from the house.

Sheila kissed his cheeks affectionately and invited him into the kitchen, where the table was set with small porcelain plates, fresh baguettes, butter, and homemade blackberry jam.

"Coffee? Or perhaps you share Benjamin's tastes?" she said, tossing her hair back. After a beat she added, "I can prepare Grand Yunnan if you like."

"Coffee, please," Virgile said, sitting down and then stiffening when Sheila scooted her chair right next to his. After a few minutes of niceties, Virgile stood up, happy to get some breathing room. He pointed to the framed photograph. "Let me get right to the point. Who is the man in that picture?"

"Why do you ask? You think he might be a boyfriend?" she said with a flirtatious smile.

"No, that's not at all what I was thinking," Virgile spat out. He immediately realized how that sounded and rushed to soften his words. "I mean I'm just curious. He looks familiar."

"Allow me to satisfy your curiosity. That's the most important man in my life."

"Oh?"

"He's my son, Nathan. Does it surprise you that I have a grown son?"

"A bit. It's just that when you told my boss about your life, you seem to have left out the part about a son. At least he didn't tell me that you had a son. I'm sure he told you about his daughter, Margaux."

"It's my life. What I share or don't share with anyone else is my own business."

"Maybe the identity of your son's father is a problem?"

"Nathan is Styron's son."

"So why all the mystery?"

"There's no mystery, Virgile. My son just happens to be the jealous type. I prefer to keep him away from any lovers I might have, and for that matter, I've never seen the need to share information about my son with those who come and go. I do admit to being an overprotective mother."

"What does he do for a living?"

"He's involved in theater, and he models to make ends meet. He studied archeology but ditched it because he wanted to act. He's in London a lot. He had a part in a musical. It closed after a short run. Sometimes he models for commercials and print ads. He's rather good looking."

"And he knows it."

"Yes, he's quite aware that he's handsome. With his looks, no one could blame him for a touch of arrogance."

"How old is he?"

"A bit older than you."

Sheila extended her right arm and reached into a pile of catalogs and magazines on the buffet. She picked up a swimwear catalog and handed it to him. On the cover was a predatory-looking model.

"What can I say? Handsome fella. Hats off."

"He looks like Styron: same eyes."

When it came to the man who had shared her life for so long, Virgile found it curious that Sheila called him only by his last name.

"Where does your Nathan live?"

"Sometimes in London, more often in Paris. He spends weeks at a time there. He's not very forthcoming about his life. He doesn't like answering questions. On the other hand, he wants to know everything about my life. As you can imagine, I take great care when I talk about myself."

"So does your son, the actor-model, make enough to live on? He never hits you up for any money?"

"Already, without knowing him, you judge him. Besides, what business is it of yours?"

"I just asked if he can get by on his own. Modeling is tough. And he looks so familiar. I'm trying to figure out where I've seen him."

"Did Benjamin send you?" she asked. She rose from her chair and edged closer to him. Her arm was brushing his. Her lips were quivering.

"No, he didn't. He's already done with Jarnac," Virgile said. He turned away and looked out the window.

"Do you still have feelings for my boss?"

"I don't know. I don't know anymore. It seems so long ago now."

"But you lured him here. You wanted to trap him. As it turns out, you didn't know him at all. My boss values loyalty. Being unfaithful is abhorrent to him. You realize that now, apparently, because you're coming on to me. So tell me why. Is it because you're desperate to make my boss jealous, or is it because you're trying to make the Lavoisier woman jealous? You're aware of her interest in me. Admit it."

"So you think this was all about some scheme I had in mind? You think I'm manipulating you to get you into my bed? Then you're the one who's ignorant. You don't know me. Get out of here! Just go!"

Virgile was already at the door.

§ § §

Lavoisier Cognacs was in the news the following week. And it was good news. Lavoisier won the gold medal at the eau-de-vie competition at the Salon de l'agriculture in Paris. The trade journals devoted several glowing articles to the woman who, through thick and thin, had succeeded in preserving the spirit of authentic cognac. In her interviews, the heiress never failed to dedicate the medal to her deceased brother, "certainly the best nose in all of Charente." The independence of Lavoisier Cognacs was no longer in question. A new French associate was by her side. As for the Chinese investors, they were simply silent partners who were keeping a watchful eye on market developments.

Benjamin dashed off a congratulatory note and was quickly rewarded with a phone call from the recipient.

"Mr. Cooker, I must thank you for your support. You have a lot to do with the recovery of our company."

"I believe you are giving me too much credit, Ms. Lavoisier."

"I know how modest you are, and I confess I was not always worthy of your trust. At any rate, it's all water under the bridge. When will you be back in Jarnac?"

"My goodness, I'll come whenever the opportunity presents itself."

"I've heard that your assistant has already been back here in Charente. He visited one of your compatriots, a certain Sheila Scott. You know about that, I presume?"

"Oh yes," the winemaker replied, swallowing his surprise.

"I did some checking. She does not have a very good reputation."

"I suppose you heard that from Mr. Fauret de Solmilhac. Is he privy to confidential information about this person?" Benjamin made his tone just condescending enough to head off any more disparaging remarks. Then the wine expert added, "Most women are careful about protecting their reputations, wouldn't you say?"

There was a moment of silence before Marie-France, all sweetness, repeated her invitation.

"Something tells me we'll be seeing each other soon," Benjamin concluded. "Call it intuition. My regards, Ms. Lavoisier." Benjamin felt himself flushing with anger. He had always tried to avoid prying into his assistant's private life. Yes, maybe Virgile was just paying Sheila an innocent visit. But he wondered if there wasn't more to it. Had Virgile lost his head and gotten involved with not only Marie-France but also his ex-lover? Benjamin didn't want to even think about it.

§ § §

When Virgile called, Marie-France's voice was flat at first but quick to become honey laced, "Oh, darling. What has become of you? Do swing by if you are in Jarnac."

Virgile borrowed the van again, and when he arrived, the sun was already leaving shadows on the landscape. The aromas of summer were floating beneath the alders, and the public garden was swarming with teenagers. The sound of excited laughter was coming from the riverbanks. The air was warm, and dragonflies were dancing on the water. Marie-France, however, was standing motionless on the landing at Château Floyras.

"Thank you for seeing me," Virgile said.

"Of course. It's always a pleasure."

"I know I was insistent, but I need to have a look at something in the greenhouse."

Marie France gazed at the Charente River as it carried petals from the wild almond tree blossoms downstream. Then she took Virgile by the wrist.

"Come," she said.

Marie-France led Virgile to the greenhouse, where Pierre Lavoisier's little world was still intact. His sister had not moved anything in this baroque setting, where each object, each piece of furniture told a story. Only the dust seemed recent. A gilded cherub holding a torch greeted the silent visitors with a smile.

"You didn't touch anything," Virgile said.

"The only thing I've done is search Pierre's desk. I've gone through every single account. I even found a secret drawer. Come see."

Marie-France Lavoisier opened the roll-top desk, pulled out the drawer, and revealed a cache of pages from a variety of catalogs. The same man was in each of them. He was affecting a pose and expression meant to make the products on the pages more appealing. He was damned good at it.

"Wow! Nathan. Yes, that's Nathan!" Virgile was sure of it.

"Who?"

"The son of..." Virgile stopped himself. "You've never seen this man at Floyras?"

"Never, I swear."

"You're sure your brother didn't have visitors here?"

"With Pierre, you could never be sure of anything."

"Why, then, when I asked you if he might have had a secret lover, didn't you say anything about it possibly being a man?"

"Be quiet! Don't tarnish his memory, I beg you."

"I was fond of your brother, and I respected him. I never would have judged him because of his sexual orientation. I won't hide the fact that he was attracted to me. He would have been more forward if I hadn't discouraged him. But that didn't keep us from being friends. He was intelligent and sensitive."

"Who is this Nathan? Do you know him? I am sure he's a gigolo. He's the one who milked him for all that money!"

"Probably," Virgile agreed.

"Do you think he killed Pierre?"

"Why would he do that?"

"I...I don't know. But you still haven't answered me. Do you know this pervert?"

"Please, don't talk like that. Pierre wouldn't want you to speak that way about any lover or friend. And I don't want you to either."

"Forgive me. I overstepped."

"I don't know this man. I just know who he is."

"You think he and my brother were..."

"At this point, we can't rule it out."

"Do you think this Nathan was holding something over Pierre?"

"Regardless of what you think, there's no stigma in being gay these days."

"You're right. What does it matter anyway?" Marie-France said, looking into the distance. "What's done is done."

Abruptly, she turned back to Virgile. "I'm a bundle of nerves. Have a drink with me."

"No, I have to get back to Bordeaux. Mr. Cooker is expecting me. We have a tasting tonight in a big château in the Médoc, and I really can't get out of it."

"Yes, I understand."

They said good-bye with a handshake, and agreeing that they felt just a little awkward, they hugged like two friends united by a secret pact. It was more than an embrace but less than a kiss, which would have led to more. Virgile needed to take his leave. He knew his weakness. He jumped into the van and took off from Floyras in a cloud of dust.

11

Chinese Investors Consider Upping Stake in Lavoisier Cognacs

A Chinese investment firm is poised to acquire even more shares of one of the oldest and most prestigious cognac companies in Jarnac, following the death of a primary owner. The Cheng Group could acquire enough shares of Lavoisier Cognacs to have equal ownership with Marie-France Lavoisier, who heads the company. Lavoisier has fought the acquisition, first made possible when her older brother, Claude-Henri, sold his shares to the Chinese firm. Now it appears that the accidental death of her younger brother, Pierre, could open the door wider.

A family ally has said he is ready to buy back shares the Cheng Group already owns. But according to Hong Kong News, *the Chinese group headed by Shiyi Cheng has no intention of selling its shares and, in fact, will move to acquire more shares, even though it would still lack controlling interest. Industry experts say the Chinese firm's*

acquisition is intriguing, as the spirits market in the
Far East is experiencing a deep recession.

Seated on the Noailles veranda, Benjamin carefully folded the salmon-colored pages of *Le Figaro* and ordered his steak with shallots, grilled just the way he liked it: rare.

"And with that, Mr. Cooker?"

"A Château la Louvière, please, and a carafe of water."

The waiter, with his Andalusian accent and legendary talkativeness, usually engaged Benjamin in friendly conversation. The wine-maker had known him since opening his offices on the Allées de Tourny. But today Benjamin was anxious and moody. Of course, this was not keeping him from fully appreciating the 1994 Louvière, with its herbaceous nose and fullness in the mouth. Benjamin slapped the thick liquid on his palate. Maybe his salvation would come from what was at the bottom of his glass, rather than what was in the papers.

Benjamin's fleeting optimism vanished when Virgile arrived on the veranda. His assistant flashed his usually irresistible smile. Benjamin, however, hadn't forgotten the troubling questions concerning his assistant's behavior.

"Have you had lunch yet?"

"No, boss, I've just left the lab. Three of our clients in Graves are fighting an invasion of dead-arm. We might have to use the radical method. Damned fungus!"

The waiter had already set Virgile's place.

"Tell me, Virgile, I don't usually meddle in your private life, but how is it going with your women in Charente?"

"What do you mean, boss?"

Much to his own surprise, Benjamin felt himself losing his proverbial British calm. "Can't you contain yourself, boy?"

"Mr. Cooker, I'm sorry, but I'm not following you. Okay, I dabbled in the cognac a little but found it a bit strong for my taste, and that was that."

"So tell me, Virgile, how is Sheila these days? I hear you paid Samson's Mill a visit. Strange— you didn't tell me you were going."

Virgile didn't miss a beat. "Oh, don't tell me you think I was up to something."

Benjamin glared at him, cleared his throat, and said in a perfectly neutral voice, "Beware of Delilah."

"Sir, please don't give it a second thought. Yes, I do have a weakness for older women, but she's not my type. And I don't think I'd get past her son, anyway. He's not keen on the idea of her having any boyfriends."

"Her son?"

"Your friend didn't bother to tell you that she had a grown son, Nathan. His father is none other than her old companion."

"Styron? The writer?"

"Yes, Styron. But I didn't know he was a writer."

"You obviously don't read a lot of fiction, Virgile. And speaking of fiction, you're saying that there's nothing between you and Sheila Scott?"

"Sir—with all due respect—you and I have shared an almost lifelong interest in wine, but we have not shared the same woman."

Benjamin looked at him without flinching and sighed. "All that is moot at this point. Sheila and I were lovers a lifetime ago. We're no more than friends now, and that's the way I want it." He wiped a dribble of wine off the bottle. It had been threatening to run onto the label, with its handsome château reflected in the water.

Virgile watched. "'Sooner or later, all the pleasures of youth come back to haunt us,' my grandfather always said."

Was this Virgile's clumsy attempt to philosophize? If so, Benjamin didn't want any part of it. "As I said, Virgile, that's all in the past. Next topic."

"Let me point out that you're the one who brought it up."

"That's true. Forgive me. How old is her son?"

"Mid-thirties. He's a frustrated actor who models for catalogs. Not too interesting in my book."

Before laying into a slice of clafoutis, Virgile told Benjamin about Nathan's affair with Pierre.

"In any case, we may be going back to Jarnac soon, my boy."

"Yes, I saw in the paper that the Chinese are upping their stake. That Fauret de Solmilhac is just a windbag if you ask me. So Marie-France is going to lose control of the company, isn't she?"

"I wouldn't be so sure," Benjamin said, smiling enigmatically.

When the waiter brought the bill, Virgile grabbed it and took out his credit card.

"Oh, come on, you don't need to do that," Benjamin said.

"Let me take care of it, boss. I've been feeling indebted to you lately."

The winemaker cracked a smile and emptied his glass of Louvière, uncapped his Havana, and watched his assistant beat a path between the tables and escape into the Allées de Tourny, where a beautiful brunette with a turned-up nose was waiting for him.

Benjamin picked up the *Le Figaro* again and started to go through the leisure section. He spotted a review of the most recent issue of the *Cooker Guide*. The critics were being particularly nitpicky this year. No one would ever admit it openly, but he suspected it was because he had doubled the chapters on North American wines.

§ § §

That night, Marie-France did not forego her moon bath. The light was warm and caressing. She stretched out on the sofa, thought of Virgile, imagined him in her brother's arms, and could not fall asleep. The following day, she had a meeting in Cognac with a lawyer named Jolliet. He had been in charge of the estate since her brother's death.

"We need to meet very quickly," the lawyer had said in a hushed voice. "Tomorrow at nine thirty will be perfect."

The lawyer's office overlooked the Charente River. From the waiting room, Marie-France could see boats with the Hennessy flag carrying sightseers across the river, where gray wine warehouses rose up like cathedrals without steeples. Marie-France watched the spectacle with the pride of a company owner who had, until now, refused any touristy compromises. Lavoisier Cognacs didn't have to go chasing after customers. Lavoisier customers, whether they were in New York, Hong Kong, Singapore, or Dubaï, were practically handpicked. But for how much longer?

Marie-France was thinking about all this when she heard the refined voice of Mr. Jolliet.

"My dear Ms. Lavoisier, always on time."

The lawyer's dark and ostentatious office was as dusty as its occupant. With his snowy hair, badly trimmed beard, and waxy complexion, the Lavoisier attorney was from another era. His bowtie almost brightened the appearance of this man, bent with age or perhaps the weight of secrets in his charge. From among the files cluttering his Napoleon III-style office, he reached for the thickest one, cinched in a purple cardboard folder.

"As you know, you and your older brother are, in fact, the only heirs. The absence of any will simplifies the procedure. Lavoisier Cognacs shares held by your deceased brother, or a little over thirty-three percent of the company, will be split between your brother, Claude-Henri, and you. Half will go to you, and half will go to him."

Mr. Jolliet paused, as if his explanation was not plain enough. He cleared his throat and added, "Do you follow me?"

"Perfectly, Mr. Jolliet."

"Your brother informed me yesterday of his intentions."

"Everyone knows his plans. I read the paper just as you do, Mr. Jolliet."

"Yes, but the paper did not say that your brother refused the offer made by a certain Maurice Fauret de Solmilhac. Furthermore, your brother rejected the Cheng group's offer to buy the shares at 2.3 million euros. Mr. Lavoisier has informed me that he does not wish to sell his shares but will henceforth sit on the board of directors of the company you manage."

Marie-France waited for an explanation of this turn of events but received none. She showed no reaction. Against all odds, the Lavoisier company, which had been up for grabs just a few days earlier, was finally safe.

"Good, good," she said simply, as though this wise decision was part of the natural order of things.

Who had convinced Claude-Henri that he shouldn't allow himself to be bought? It had to be the prime minister's envoy. Marie-France felt like a pawn in the chess game of her life.

Standing before the decrepit lawyer, she pretended that she had arranged the whole thing. With a shaky hand, she signed the documents.

12

"Will you stop by the mill for a cup of tea?"

"I'm afraid I don't have time," Benjamin Cooker said firmly. "I'd rather meet in Jarnac, if that's okay. On the island in the public gardens."

"That sounds a little like a romantic rendez-vous," Sheila said. "Have you been in the gazebo?"

"The gazebo will do just fine," the winemaker said a little conspiratorially.

The Englishwoman giggled and promised to be there at five o'clock, no earlier.

The gazebo wasn't the ornate, nostalgic type seen on many town squares, but rather a modern little building with benches where people could sit and watch the impetuous or languid waters of the Charente, depending on the season.

Carved on the benches were obscenities, along with hearts with initials. At night, the gazebo was the scene of surreptitious meetings, furtive embraces, forbidden affairs, and sighs and groans barely masked by the splash of fish and the rustling of bats. With the river as the only witness and a forest of shrubs as a screen, it was a perfect setting for illicit lovemaking.

During the day, however, there were only runners in jogging outfits, occasional fishermen, and lonely souls who came to dream in a corner of nature protected from the tribulations of the rest of the world.

Sheila Scott was late. Benjamin used the time to jot down some notes about the vintages he had tasted the night before. His old friend was in a sweat when she finally arrived. She was wearing a white linen sundress that hardly flattered her milky skin.

"Why the devil did you make me come here? It's charming and all, but not very reassuring for a woman who's alone."

"What are you afraid of? A werewolf, a wild animal, or a handsome boy ready to woo you?"

Sheila stiffened and stared at the riverbank.

"Why didn't you tell me that you have a son?"

"A certain taste for privacy, perhaps."

"When you have a handsome kid, you don't deny yourself the pleasure of showing him off," Benjamin said, stretching his legs out to savor the sun's soft rays.

"How do you know about him?" Sheila asked. Benjamin could tell she was taking umbrage.

"I think he sells his image."

"He makes a living at it. He gets by."

"Yes, I'm sure his looks help him get by. But something tells me that he needs more than those modeling jobs. He has an income stream or two on the side."

"What are you insinuating?"

"I saw the kind of car he drives."

"Benjamin, what are getting at? What exactly do you want to know?"

"For the sake of the old and intimate times we shared, I'd like to hear from your lips what I already know."

"But I don't owe you anything, especially not any explanations! Our paths wouldn't have crossed again if we hadn't had that chance meeting on the terrace of the Coq d'Or."

"You are absolutely right. Providence, however, put us together on that terrace. Unless, of course, you arranged it all. I understand that you want to protect your son, but in a few hours, he will be taken in for questioning and possibly charged with murder."

"Murder?"

Sheila tried to meet Benjamin's eyes. Confronted with his hard stare, she looked away and walked over to the railing of the gazebo. Benjamin followed.

"Why did you pretend that you didn't know the Lavoisiers?"

"You call that knowing? Everyone here knows everyone else. Marie-France is just an arrogant and conniving woman who cries crocodile tears about being eaten alive by the big-money Chinese. We know how that worked out. Well done! Claude-Henri is no better, but at least he's never been one to go around complaining. As for the brother they buried, he was just a manic-depressive who never felt good about himself."

"And your son consoled him as best he could."

"Yes, I think they knew each other."

"You might even say they were intimate."

"What are you trying to get me to say?"

"Nothing that isn't true," Benjamin said, skipping a stone over the water like a bored child killing time.

"Yes, they got on well with each other. Pierre Lavoisier was a bit of an artist, a sensitive type, and Nathan liked him a lot. They enjoyed spending time together."

"Indeed, they were very close," Benjamin said.

"You want me to say that my son is gay? Well, you're wrong!"

"I don't care whether he's gay or not. That's his business. But he has the profile of a rather brilliant and unscrupulous young man who demanded money from his friend, lover—whatever—and damned big amounts at that, so that he could live the life his mother couldn't provide for him. He most likely told Pierre, who was already depressed, that he would leave if he didn't come up with the cash. Maybe the threat was always hanging over Pierre's head."

"That's not true!"

"He'll have to prove it. Not to me, but to the cops."

"Nathan isn't that underhanded, and he's certainly no murderer."

"The evidence has accumulated over the last few weeks, and the guy who started the investigation is a young man who is very charming himself. Beauty is not always the promise of happiness, contrary to what Stendhal said."

"Spare me your stupid quotations, please!"

"If you weren't the woman I held in my arms so long ago, I wouldn't be here."

"Well, go ahead. Run to the police, and tell your lies. Drag my son through the mud."

Benjamin went back to the graffiti-covered bench and sat down. A robin landed nearby and pecked at a bread crumb left by a passerby. On the opposite bank, the towers of Château Floyras rose above the trees.

"Come and sit down."

"Why?" Sheila asked. She pulled a tissue out of her handbag.

"Come here, I said."

Sheila went over and sat down. She put her head on Benjamin's shoulder, just as she had on that spring day when the hailstorm tore through the garden.

They almost looked liked lovers.

§ § §

Benjamin Cooker had arranged to meet his assistant at the train station café that night. "Take the first train. I'll pick you up in Angoulême, because the connection for Cognac is too late." After all the bad luck, the worst predictions regarding the future of the Lavoisier business, and the wild gossip, Benjamin planned to get to the bottom of Pierre Lavoisier's death. Was it accidental or intentional? A bad fall, a fit of dizziness on the bank of the Charente could happen so easily. But then again, it wasn't hard to imagine an angry or even deliberate push.

"I didn't expect to be making another trip to Jarnac this soon," Virgile declared as he jumped off the train.

"I do hope it will be the last," Benjamin grumbled.

The winemaker spared his assistant no details of his argument in the gazebo with the woman who even now hoped to be his mistress. Sheila had denied that Nathan would ever lean on Pierre for extravagant sums of money, but she had confirmed their friendship. And as far as she was concerned, that was all that it was: a friendship.

"The woman knows nothing about her son. She still considers him as innocent as a choirboy," Benjamin said.

"But maybe he's just an unscrupulous gigolo and not a murderer. I can't figure out his motive. Why would he eliminate the very person who was signing over one check after another?"

"You're right, Virgile. This Nathan is the lynch-pin of our mystery, but even though I've never met him, I don't see how he could be completely unlikable. Knowing his mother and having read his father's books, I have to believe that Nathan has some redeeming qualities."

"Listen, Sheila's son may have one or two redeeming qualities, but one thing is sure: he's shady. He's never around but seems to take up a lot of space."

"You can say that again," Benjamin mumbled.

"Are we staying at Château Yeuse?"

"Yes, why?" Benjamin asked.

"Because with your permission, I'd like to go to Samson's Mill to have a little talk with our top model. I'd like to see what this guy who's been lining his pockets for so long is hiding in his shorts, if you get my meaning."

"I know you, Virgile. You'll come to blows."

"All brawn and no brains, my grandmother used to say."

"I don't think it's very wise, Virgile."

"In this matter, nothing is really wise. Who would think that the son of your first love…I assume you couldn't be his father, right?"

Benjamin couldn't help smiling. His assistant continued. "Really, this is all very complicated. Who would believe it if we told them the story? Here we are, stuck in a corner of fucking Charente, investigating a drowning that could be a murder, involved with an elite but peculiar family, and trying to extricate ourselves from a sticky situation with a woman with a passion for roses, among other things—after taking on and dropping a job commissioned by a client halfway around the world."

Benjamin Cooker smoothed his hair and offered to buy his assistant a beer. He wanted to rein in the thoughts racing through his head.

But sitting across from each other at the laminate table, they hardly spoke. Benjamin was thinking of Sheila. He wanted to pull the thorn from her side. The rose grower's son would surely be investigated. It was only a matter of hours. Benjamin spent several minutes advising Virgile before giving him the keys to the convertible. His main concern was not so much his treasured Mercedes, but rather the confrontation with Sheila's son.

"Leave your cell phone on. I want to be able to reach you the whole time. Understand?"

"Okay, boss! Worst-case scenario, Nathan isn't there, and I spend the night at the mill with our lady love," Virgile said with a wink.

Benjamin did not appreciate his stab at humor.
"No nonsense, son!" he said in parting.

§ § §

Like an elegant Venetian mirror, the water reflected the radiance of Samson's Mill in the vio-
let-colored night. A chorus of crickets was rising
from the garden, which emanated the intoxicating fragrances of Sheila's roses. In the distance, the
church of Villars-les-Bois was like a lighthouse in
a swell of grapevines.

Virgile had parked the convertible on the
road from Migron to avoid arousing Sheila and
Nathan's curiosity. Through one of the windows,
he could see them sitting at the table. He rang the
bell, turned up the collar of his jacket, and slipped
his hands into the back pockets of his jeans. He
recognized Sheila's steps and voice. "At this time
of night?"

"Oh, hey, it's you. I mean, good evening."
Nathan's mother feigned surprise as she let Virgile
in. She stumbled through an inarticulate intro-
duction, her lips trembling.

"Nathan, this...This...is Virgile, the son of your
father's friend. You remember. I told you about him."

With a sullen look, Nathan studied the visitor
who had emerged from the darkness. Still sitting

in his chair, he struck a pose. Virgile assumed he intended to look provocative, but that didn't quite come across. A poor actor, Virgile thought. His tone was just as false.

"Styron never mentioned you or your dad," he said.

"And for good reason," Virgile replied. He was watching Sheila's drawn face and tired eyes. "I am nobody's son here. And I'm certainly not the son of some distant friend. My so-called dad is a much more intimate acquaintance of your mother's."

"Get out of here!"

"So Sheila didn't tell you anything."

"Go to hell!"

Nathan stood up. His build was more impressive than the catalog photos suggested. He easily could have been on a rugby team in Bergerac. Not as a forward, of course, but as a wing, for sure.

Sheila's son looked threatening, but his quavering voice betrayed his anxiety.

"I think we need to talk, the two of us," Virgile said.

"I have nothing to say to you. Get lost!"

"Stop the bullshit. I don't know you, but I won't beat around the bush. You're used to that, I'm sure. You get on familiar terms real quick, don't you?"

Nathan's expression changed. Virgile could tell he was no longer playing the role of the belligerent child but was looking to his mother for an explanation.

"You're going to listen to me," Virgile insisted, "and play fair, or else you're screwed."

"Mom, who is this cretin? Who does he think he is?"

"Listen to him, for God's sake," she responded. Sheila was already crying.

"Sheila, Nathan and I need to sit down and have a talk. Can you make us some coffee? Nathan, I know you're looking for celebrity, and in forty-eight hours, in my opinion, you're going to be on the front page of the newspapers. At least the *Sud-Ouest* and *La Charente Libre*. But it won't be the kind of notoriety you're looking for."

"What are you talking about?"

"Either you take me for a fool, or you don't understand that you've been living on borrowed time. Let's start at the beginning. I believe you were a friend, a great friend or, more likely, a boyfriend of Pierre Lavoisier."

"That's none of your business! My private life is—"

"Yes, I know. Your private life is your own business. But if you had feelings for Pierre, why weren't you at his funeral?"

"I had an audition for a television commercial."

"And your friendship wasn't more important than a stupid commercial?"

"My work isn't stupid."

"To the contrary, I have high regard for what you do. I know how important it is and how busy you are. As a matter of fact, I was hoping you would tell me you were shooting a commercial in some distant country on the night that Pierre jumped—or fell—into the water, because that would remove the suspicion hanging over you."

"What suspicion? What are you implying? Sure, Pierre was a friend. More than that. He was the person I could always talk to about anything. And I could count on him."

"He was something of a big brother, wasn't he? A father, too."

"Maybe, even though I didn't really think of him that way."

Nathan was now himself, Virgile thought: fragile, vulnerable, obviously sensitive. He refused the cup of coffee his mother handed him and fumbled as he tried to light a cigarette.

"Could I have a cognac, please, Mom? But first, tell him. Go ahead, tell him that Pierre was my friend. Shit, tell him!" He looked at Virgile. "You're accusing me of what—killing him?"

"I'm not accusing you of anything, but in Pierre Lavoisier's desk they found tangible proof that you regularly fleeced him."

"Me? I fleeced him?"

"Don't tell us any of your lies, Nathan. We have to know, your mother and I."

His eyes fixed on the amber-colored cognac, Sheila's son rationalized his friend's generosity, saying that it seemed perfectly acceptable, not at all excessive, just something a close friend was doing from the goodness of his heart.

"Sometimes Pierre would give me presents, mostly clothes. One of his nicest presents was this watch. It's an old Lip, and I love it. I wear it all the time. But I never needed any of his dough. I do okay on my own. What do you take me for? A gigolo, a prostitute?"

Nathan had not even put the cognac Sheila had poured to his lips. The flask had no label. Just a piece of tape that read: "Sample for Nathan, 1979." Virgile recognized Pierre Lavoisier's handwriting. Hadn't he himself received, in a gesture of friendship not devoid of ambiguity, a flask blended in his year of birth?

Virgile watched as tears trickled down Nathan's cheeks. Styron's son couldn't forgive himself for missing Pierre's funeral. Yes, he was a bastard, an ingrate, the lowest of the low...Then taking his accuser aside, he murmured in a sweet and clear voice, "But why would I have done anything to harm him?"

Virgile glanced at Sheila. The answer to that question had the power to absolve him or condemn him.

"Pierre loved me more than I could love him. But he never held that against me."

"You know, that's the way it often is with love," Virgile said. "There's one person who loves more than the other."

Virgile looked at Sheila again and saw that she had emptied Nathan's glass of cognac. Had she downed it in a single gulp? Virgile saw her try to put the glass on the table. She missed. The glass shattered on the floor the very second she collapsed on the faded yellow couch.

§ § §

When Benjamin's assistant left them, the moon was casting a dull light on the motionless paddles of the water mill. Virgile did not put the convertible top up. The air was warm and smelled of heather.

At Château Yeuse, Benjamin was sitting in the library. Enveloped in plumes of gray smoke, he was taking great delight in a Montecristo A with an oily cap. As soon as he spotted Virgile, he rewarded him with a cheerful grin that clearly said, "I was expecting you."

"Would you like to have a Lavoisier? Taste this 1982, my dear Virgile."

13

Salt-and-pepper hair, impeccably cut, deep tan, blue shirt and caramel-colored cashmere sweater, the proud bearing and elegant movements: Claude-Henri Lavoisier belonged to a certain breed of flamboyant men. He wore his years gracefully and did not seem the least bit tired from his eight-hour transatlantic flight. He arrived at night with no warning, almost like a thief.

Marie-France was not asleep. The waning crescent moon was keeping her company. Twice she asked the night visitor to identify himself before she opened the Château Floyras gates. Who would show up at this hour? But even in the darkest night, she would have recognized her brother. Time and distance had not erased the memory of that arrogant silhouette.

"Claude? Is it you? What are you doing here?"

"Well, as you can see, I'm back in the country. Am I still welcome?"

"Of course! Come in."

The taxi driver was waiting for his money. Claude-Henri had only a Visa card and a fistful of Canadian dollars. Marie-France hastened to pay the fare. No, he hadn't changed. No, he wasn't hungry. No, he had no other bags.

"I can't believe you're really here after all this time. Can I touch you to make sure I'm not seeing things? Are you wearing the same cologne?"

Marie-France patted his wrists, his sides, and his chest to confirm that she wasn't dreaming. During her moon baths, she had often imagined the day her Claude would come home for good. And here he was, smiling, beaming, loving.

"Are you thirsty?"

"No, but I wouldn't turn down a Lavoisier."

The sister rushed to the cabinet beneath the Chinese tapestry in the Floyras breakfast room. This piece of furniture was from an old dispensary on the Rue de Condé. Pierre had salvaged it after the elderly pharmacist, Guilhem, had put cyanide in his ratatouille to end the agony of throat cancer. On the upper shelves were stoneware pots bearing Latin names. In the center, in small sepia-colored bottles, were all the Lavoisier vintages since the founding of the company. Two centuries of cognac graced this display cabinet. Marie-France took one of the vials, the lightest in color. The cork slipped out with a sinister squeak, and she quietly confessed, "This is Pierre's last blend. Full of finesse and subtlety. Taste it."

Claude-Henri warmed the glass in his hand, as if putting off the moment of communion with this little brother, who had gone to heaven without getting even a good-bye wave. He was angry with himself for missing the funeral. He had been in Vancouver when his associate informed him of Pierre's death, and there wasn't enough time to get to Jarnac.

"I should have written or called. I behaved like the most egotistical and stupid jerk. But you know, my life in Canada, all the real estate deals I brokered, all the money I made, it just did one thing for me..."

Marie-France poured herself a bit of the cognac that had won the gold medal in Paris. She swirled her glass to watch the full-bodied liquid run in tiny rivulets down the sides. A fine fragrance of apricot and yellow peach caressed her nostrils.

"It made me realize how much I missed Jarnac and how much I missed you. And living far from the Charente is impossible for me."

"So you're not going back to Montreal?"

"No, Marie-France, it's over. I'm staying here. That is, if it's okay with you."

"God, how silly you can be sometimes!"

Brother and sister drank to the last blends Pierre had produced, which, year after year, had been the best cognacs of Grande Champagne. By now Claude-Henri was sobbing, Marie curled up

141

on the sofa and pulled her Shetland-wool sweater over her knees. She watched her brother tenderly. Finally, she was not alone. Nothing bad could happen to her.

"I'll move into the greenhouse. I don't want to bother you or disturb your life in any way."

"No, you will live in the château. With me."

"As you wish."

Then the two remaining Lavoisiers fell into each other's arms, as they had during haymaking season when they were children. They had rolled in the bales and laughed until they couldn't breathe. When the sun's rays broke through the château windows at dawn, spreading the aromas of truffles and ripening peaches, brother and sister were still entwined.

That evening they would celebrate the feast of Saint John the Baptist and the summer solstice. The laughter of boaters on the Charente was already drifting up from the park.

Marie-France asked Justine to serve breakfast on the terrace. "Quince jelly and fig jam, please." The sun was as sweet as honey, and she intended to indulge. She was wearing a T-shirt that seductively hugged her breasts and bore the company slogan: "Cognac Lavoisier: Of course you deserve it!"

The aroma of coffee lured Claude-Henri out of his torpor. Though still fatigued from jet lag, he said he was starving. "What time is it?" he asked.

"At least nine o'clock."

"Perfect. Can we add a cup to the table? I invited our new consultant to have breakfast with us."

"A consultant? What's this nonsense?"

"Last night, I completely forgot to tell you that I liquidated all my assets in Canada. Yes, Marie-France, I've sold everything. Cashed out. With the little nest egg the sale of my assets generated and on the strong recommendation of my new consultant in France, I purchased the shares your Asians held—at thirty percent less than what they paid for them. You don't need to teach a man from Charente how to use an abacus! I think they decided to throw in the towel because of the financial crisis hitting the Far East. I dealt with a man named Guo Liang. Do you know him?"

"Never heard of him."

"Cheng was fired, though I'm sure he left with a tidy little sum of his own."

Shocked by the news, Marie-France spilled her coffee.

"Do you have anything else to tell me?"

"The best is still to come, Marie-France!"

"You know I love you, right?"

Brother and sister embraced in front of a wide-eyed Justine, who would not fail to alert all of Jarnac about the powerful duo now presiding over Lavoisier Cognacs. Justine Pergaut had been in the family's employ for more than thirty years and had stood by during the glory years, as well as those that were full of misfortune.

A roaring engine interrupted the happy mood scented with jams, which were now drawing honeybees from the surrounding bushes.

"Well, here's our new consultant right now!" Claude-Henri exclaimed.

"My respects, Ms. Lavoisier. I was absolutely convinced that we would see each other very soon," Benjamin said with a sly grin.

"Marie-France, you can thank Benjamin Cooker for my return. I was wallowing in guilt over missing Pierre's farewell when he called and convinced me we could still honor our family heritage."

§ § §

That day, Benjamin Cooker enjoyed some of the sweetest moments of his profession. He was invited to sample the amber treasures that decorated the dispensary shelves. In a tasting orchestrated by Marie-France and Claude-Henri, he discovered the diverse aromas that dominated Little Pierre's brandies. He took in the scents of pear, apple, kirsch, cherry, strawberry, cranberry, fig, apricot, plum, quince, muscat, lemon, orange, grapefruit, citron, and Mirabelle plums. He wafted fragrances of violet, mint, verbena, fern, moss, anise, fennel, linden, gentian, angelica, tobacco, lavender, and mushroom, along with some spicy aromas, including cinnamon, pepper, clove, ginger, nutmeg, licorice, and saffron.

"Your brother's oldest cognacs smell of wild animals, don't you think?" Benjamin said. "Fur, leather, civet, and musk."

He could see that Claude-Henri was also discovering an entire paradise of enchanting fragrances. It was as if he knew nothing about the cognac world, even though he had grown up in the midst of it.

As the black, green, and blood-red wax stoppers were ceremoniously doffed, Benjamin displayed his extensive knowledge.

"Dried-fruit and nutty aromas predominate in many of your distillations: almond, walnut, prune, hazelnut, pistachio, sometimes even peanut. However, your brother had a penchant for citrus fruit. His cognacs smell like lemon, orange, mandarin, grapefruit, and sometimes citron."

Marie-France compared her impressions and intuitions with Benjamin's, which were indisputable. This blend had aromas of coffee, cacao, toast, flint, tea, or even tar. That blend gave off fragrances of butter, caramel, hot sand, hummus, or beeswax.

The winemaker continued. "But the most beautiful Lavoisier relics have woody notes: rancio, of course, oak, tropical wood, and unseasoned, even resinous, wood."

The entire morning was devoted to tasting and envisioning the glorious future of Lavoisier Cognac. The company would tap into an ample foreign market. Claude-Henri would take advantage of his North American connections. Every decent restaurant in Quebec, Montreal, Toronto, and Vancouver would insist on serving Lavoisier. Claude-Henri also knew influential people in Manhattan and Boston. They would hit the Russian market, too: Saint Petersburg and especially Moscow. And they would not forget about China and Japan, where the brand now had a serious reputation. The future was full of promise. Benjamin relished the excitement he could see in the eyes of the brother and sister. The two of them invoked Pierre as a sort of guardian angel who would guide new blends every year.

"Justine! Mr. Cooker is joining us for lunch. Set another place."

"Yes, ma'am. By the way, I cleaned the greenhouse, just as you asked me to. I vacuumed everywhere and washed the windows. And look what I found under your brother's desk. An old cigar box held together with rubber bands. I didn't open it."

"That was wise, Justine. Thank you. Put it on the coffee table."

"It's strange. Mr. Lavoisier didn't smoke cigars," Justine said.

"Yes, he did, I think, on occasion," Marie-France responded.

From his chair, Benjamin was inspecting the box, labeled "Château Latour." He had quickly identified it. This was a rare box that had once contained Coronas known for their excellent craftsmanship. These cigars had been created by Zino Davidoff in the nineteen forties and were manufactured in Cuba by Hoyo de Monterrey. Davidoff, who knew the reputation of Bordeaux wines, sold the exceptional cigars in five boxes labeled "Château Margaux," "Château Haut-Brion," "Château Lafite," "Château Latour," and "Château Yquem." Unfortunately, when the Davidoff company was kicked off the island in 1993 after a falling-out with Fidel Castro, production of the châteaux boxes and cigars ended.

Benjamin hoped to find a few old Coronas in this box. Aged Davidoffs, even those that were decades old, were said to be some of the finest, cleanest-smoking cigars a connoisseur could ever lay his hands on.

"May I?" Benjamin asked.

"Please," Marie-France said, holding out the dusty cedar box.

With the eyes of a child, Benjamin handled the box as if it contained the Holy Grail. After removing the two rubber bands, he opened it. The contents were covered with a cedar leaf that had a thumb index, in accordance with the packaging of the best Havanas. Benjamin removed the cover and frowned. The tobacco odor had gone stale and for good reason. There were no cigars in the box.

What Benjamin found was an odd collection. There was a program for a play in London. The winemaker looked inside and found Nathan's name in a listing of the cast. Benjamin picked up a postcard with a picture of the iconic double-decker bus. He turned it over and read the message: "Sorry you missed me. The production was fabulous." Underneath the program and postcard were three photo-booth pictures of Nathan and Pierre, a smiling couple. And there was a receipt for a 1,200-euro bottle of men's perfume: Annick Goutal's Eau d'Hadrien. Of course Pierre had purchased this for his companion. Its scents were Sicilian lemon, mandarin orange, grapefruit, citron, cypress, and extracts of a plant grown in Madagascar. Finally, there was a letter. The envelope bore a stylized rose.

Not wanting to appear too indiscreet, he handed the box to Marie-France while he skimmed the letter.

See you Thursday evening, as we agreed, at the causeway mills. I have bled myself dry for Nathan. You are well aware that he is having a difficult time and needs more than what I can provide. Your financial support is crucial, even urgent. If you ever loved my son, you will do this one thing. And if that's not enough to persuade you, let me make it clear that both Nathan and I are aware of your liaison with your sister. Talk is one thing. Proof is quite another.

Benjamin gave Marie-France the letter, the harbinger of Little Pierre's death. He asked to be excused and headed toward the terrace. When he reached the Charente, he had just enough strength to sit on a bench near the landing and watch the river spread its murky waters toward the causeway.

§ § §

When Benjamin burst into Sheila's rose garden, she was focused on a Cardinal de Richelieu, an old garden rose with mauvish-purple double flowers. Armed with pruning shears, she was fiercely snipping away, paying the sneaky thorns no mind.

"Maybe you were expecting Virgile?"

"Oh, him. I haven't heard from Virgile since the night he came over here and caused a scene with Nathan. He practically accused Nathan of killing Pierre Lavoisier."

There was something intoxicating about Sheila's roses that the winemaker, with so keen a sense of smell, found especially provocative. He took his friend by the wrist and unceremoniously drew her away from her bushes, which were getting more attention than necessary.

"What manners! You used to be more polite."

"Tell me, that meeting at the mill with Pierre Lavoisier, was it polite? I don't think so. I think it was confrontational. Don't deny it. I know everything now: how your son was using Pierre, taking advantage of his depression, and how you were whispering in Nathan's ear the whole time. I have records of the amounts, the dates, and the threats."

"Let me go. You're hurting me!"

Benjamin held Sheila's wrist tight, hoping she would give up. She struggled, and as she fought his hold, her clothes became tangled in the thorns of the rose bushes. Benjamin did not let go, and yet he held back. It wouldn't have taken much to overpower this body he had desired for so long, this woman, who was now at his knees. She was weeping but would not confess. Nathan intervened.

"What are you doing to my mother, you moron? Let her go, or I'll break your face!"

"Nathan. Don't concern yourself with this. Go away, please!" Sheila yelled to her son, who, despite his threat, made no move to take on the winemaker.

"No, Nathan, I think you should stay. After all, it was your greed that caused this, wasn't it? Your mother, living on her inheritance, couldn't give you everything you thought you were entitled to, so you exploited and manipulated Pierre. He loved you, and what did he get in return? An arrogant man who wasn't worthy of him."

Sheila Scott stopped fighting. The thorns had lacerated her arms and face, and she was panting.

"Get up," Benjamin ordered. "First, tell your son who I am. Tell him about Paris, the Beaux-Arts, and all the rest. Your son should know about your past, your list of lovers, long and varied, up until just a few months ago, when you tried to compromise my own assistant, a naïve womanizer whose brain is in his boxer shorts. Go ahead, Sheila. Tell him before he hears it from the authorities."

Nathan Styron helped his mother off the ground and watched as she straightened her clothing. Her dress was ripped and stained with mud. The scratches on her arms and face were oozing blood. Benjamin pulled out his handkerchief, but Nathan pushed him away before he could hand it to Sheila. Nathan pulled out his own handkerchief and dried her tears and wiped away the blood.

"What is he saying, Mother?"

Sheila then confessed, slipping from French to English and then back to French.

"I knew Nathan was taking money from Pierre and threatening to leave if he didn't keep the checks coming. Pierre had finally had enough. He told Nathan not to expect any more money. He could go ahead and leave. But Nathan needed the money. He was planning to move to the United States. I asked Pierre to meet me. I wanted to explain that Nathan just needed a little boost in his career, and then he could stand on his own two feet. But when Pierre got there, he reeked of alcohol. He had been drinking. He called me a pimp and other names, too. By this time he was shouting and getting too close. It scared me, and I pushed him away. He fell into the river. I think he hit his head. I didn't hear him scream. Nothing...Just the deafening sound of the water."

Sheila collapsed in tears on a carpet of rose petals. Her chest was heaving beneath the bodice of her frayed dress. The rose gardener had never looked so desirable. Benjamin cut through the garden to get to the landline in the house. He called his assistant.

"Virgile, I guessed right. Sheila is definitely not the sort of person we want to be seen with. Oh, by the way, before I get back to Bordeaux, think about this saying by Jules Renard: 'It is not the rose that draws the bird to the rosebush, but the aphids.'"

EPILOGUE

Sentenced by the Court of Angoulême to eight years in prison for manslaughter, Sheila Scott is writing a guide for rose growers, which the London publisher Huston expects to release next year. Nathan Styron is writing erotic novels and just made the cover of *Vanity Fair*. In an interview in the *Times,* the son of the famous writer said he intends to give up modeling to devote himself to intellectual pursuits. In Migron, Samson's Mill was sold to an allegedly dissolute Parisian antiquarian. Meanwhile, Lavoisier Cognacs has been restored to its former status and is a financial success. Marie-France and Claude-Henri continue to reside at Château Floyras. Many in Jarnac say that brother and sister live together as husband and wife. It is well known that the waters of the Charente have always been troubled.

§ § §

Benjamin removed Bacchus's leash and walked into the kitchen. They had just returned from their morning walk. Elisabeth was at the window, gazing at the garden. Benjamin went over to her and kissed the nape of her neck. It had always been one of the most exquisite parts of her body.

"I'm thinking about redoing the garden," she said, smiling at her husband and pointing to a spot to their right. "Maybe pulling up that part of it and planting some roses. Maybe tea roses. What do you think?"

"Hmm. Maybe we should drive into Bordeaux this weekend and take a walk through the botanical garden for inspiration. I'm thinking we should plant something else, something beautiful and rare. Like you, my love."

Thank you for reading Cognac Conspiracies.

We invite you to share your thoughts and reactions on your favorite social media and retail platforms.

We appreciate your support.

THE WINEMAKER DETECTIVE SERIES

A total epicurean immersion in French countryside and gourmet attitude with two expert winemakers turned amateur sleuths gumshoeing around wine country. The following titles are currently available in English.

Treachery in Bordeaux

This journey to Bordeaux takes readers behind the scenes of a grand cru wine estate that has fallen victim to either negligence or sabotage. Winemaker turned gentleman detective Benjamin Cooker sets out to find out what happened and why. Who would want to target this esteemed estate?

www.treacheryinbordeaux.com

Grand Cru Heist

Benjamin Cooker's world gets turned upside down one night in Paris and he retreats to the region around Tours to recover. There, a flamboyant British dandy, a spectacular blue-eyed blonde, a zealous concierge, and touchy local police disturb his well-deserved rest. The Winemaker Detective and his assistant Virgile turn PI to solve two murders and a very particular heist. Who stole those bottles of grand cru classé?

www.grandcruheist.com

Nightmare in Burgundy

The Winemaker Detective leaves his native Bordeaux to go to Burgundy for a dream wine-tasting trip. Between Beaune, Dijon and Nuits-Saint-Georges, the excursion becomes a nightmare when he stumbles upon a mystery revolving around messages from another era. What do they mean? What dark secrets from the deep past are haunting the Clos de Vougeot? Does blood need to spill to sharpen people's memory?

www.nightmareinburgundy.com

Deadly Tasting

A serial killer stalks Bordeaux. To understand the wine-related symbolism, the local police call on the famous wine critic Benjamin Cooker. The investigation leads them to the dark hours of France's history, as the mystery thickens among the once-peaceful vineyards of Pomerol.

www.deadlytasting.com

ABOUT THE AUTHORS

Noël Balen (left) and Jean-Pierre Alaux (right).
(©David Nakache)

Jean-Pierre Alaux and **Noël Balen** came up with the Winemaker Detective over a glass of wine, of course. Jean-Pierre Alaux is a magazine, radio, and television journalist when he is not writing novels in southwestern France. He is a genuine wine and food lover, and won the Antonin Carême prize for his cookbook *La Truffe sur le Soufflé*, which he wrote with the chef Alexis Pélissou. He is the grandson of a winemaker and exhibits a real passion for wine and winemaking. For him, there is no greater common denominator than wine. Coauthor of the series Noël Balen lives in Paris, where he shares his time between writing, making records, and lecturing on music. He plays bass, is a music critic, and has authored a number of books about musicians, in addition to his novel and short-story writing.

ABOUT THE TRANSLATOR

Sally Pane studied French at State University of New York Oswego and the Sorbonne before receiving her Masters Degree in French Literature from the University of Colorado. Her career includes more than twenty years of translating and teaching French and Italian at Berlitz and at University of Colorado Boulder. She has worked in scientific, legal and literary translation; her literary translations include *Operatic Arias; Singers Edition*, and *Reality and the Untheorizable* by Clément Rosset, along with a number of titles in the Winemaker Detective series. She also served as the interpreter for the government cabinet of Rwanda and translated for Dian Fossey's Digit Fund. In addition to her passion for French, she has studied Italian. She lives in Boulder, Colorado, with her husband.

Discover more books from
Le French Book
www.lefrenchbook.com

Shadow Ritual by E. Giacometti & J. Ravenne
Ritual murders. Ancient enemies. A powerful secret. In an electrifying thriller about the rise of extremism, two slayings—one in Rome and one in Jerusalem—rekindle an ancient rivalry between modern-day secret societies for knowledge lost at the fall of the Third Reich. Detective Antoine Marcas unwillingly teams up with the strong-willed Jade Zewinski to chase Neo-Nazi assassins across Europe. They must unravel an arcane Freemason mystery, sparked by information from newly revealed KGB files.
www.shadowritual.com

The Paris Homicide series by Frédérique Molay
Edge-of-your-seat mysteries set in Paris, where beautiful sounding names surround ugly crimes that have Chief of Police Nico Sirsky and his team on tenterhooks.
www.parishomicide.com

The Paris Lawyer by Sylvie Granotier
A psychological thriller set between the sophisticated corridors of Paris and a small backwater in central France, where rolling hills and quiet country life hide dark secrets.
www.theparislawyer.com

The Greenland Breach **by Bernard Besson**
The Arctic ice caps are breaking up. Europe and the
East Coast of the United States brace for a tidal wave. A
team of freelance spies face a merciless war for control of
discoveries that will change the future of humanity.
www.thegreenlandbreach.com

Consortium thrillers by David Khara
A roller-coaster ride into the history of World War II,
racing through a modern-day loop-to-loop of action.
www.theconsortiumthrillers.com

CPSIA information can be obtained at www.ICGtesting.com
Printed in the USA
BVOW08s0944030215

386016BV00005B/9/P